The Wind's Will

a novel by
Nancy Vance Cooley

PublishAmerica
Baltimore

First printing

ISBN: 1-59129-687-0
PUBLISHED BY PUBLISHAMERICA BOOK PUBLISHERS
www.publishamerica.com
Baltimore

Printed in the United States of America

A boy's will is the wind's will,
And the thoughts of youth are long, long thoughts.
-Henry Wadsworth Longfellow

For my husband John, my number one fan,
and my daughters Karen and Paula.

In memory of my grandmother Mattie Cathey,
who instilled in me an interest in Texas history,
and my mother Isola Vance,
who nurtured and supported me.

FOREWORD

Along the far-flung Texas frontier in the 1860s scattered white settlers mingled with Indians and Mexicans. Life was hazardous, often brief. Close proximity within large families in small quarters short on privacy, plus the absence of formal school requirements, resulted in early marriages and adult responsibilities for young people now considered adolescents. Marriages between teens might result from romantic attachments, but second marriages were likely arrangements of convenience between widowed fathers with families to rear and unattached females without a livelihood.

Religion was dispensed by saddlebags preachers such as the Rev. William "Choctaw Bill" Robinson (1809-1898), whom I have involved in the plot of *The Wind's Will*. Robinson during his lifetime traveled the frontier, preaching, debating denominational doctrines, and baptizing, marrying and burying settlers.

The characters (other than Robinson and several historical figures mentioned in passing) exist only in the author's imagination. The fictional Sam Gossett has been made an observer of certain colorful events in Robinson's life which are a matter of record, and Robinson has been given an imagined part in the life of the Gossetts. Some adventures experienced by the fictional characters are based on stories of frontier life handed down from the author's great grandmother, Mary Jane Robinson, who was Choctaw Bill's daughter-in-law, and from her daughter, Mattie Cathey.

Several places mentioned in the story are today a mecca for visitors. Both the Vereins Kirche in Fredericksburg and restored Ft. Croghan are Texas tourist attractions. First Monday Trade Days in Canton began in the 1850s when a circuit judge passed through Canton the first Monday of each month and farmers brought goods, produce and livestock to sell or trade. Currently First Monday Trade Days in Canton attract 2.5 million visitors annually and provide the venue for the largest flea market in the country, offering some 70 acres of merchandise and animals for sale.

Chapter 1
TWO TEEN BRIDES

"Don't you dare cry!" Sam Houston Gossett whispered to his 14-year old twin, Rose Lucille, whose misty eyes threatened a deluge of tears. At the same time he motioned with his thumb toward their younger siblings and shook his head.

James Bowie, Polly Sue, Stephen Austin, Davy Crockett, and Ruth Ellen Gossett, ranging in age from 9 years down to 18 months, huddled beneath a pile of quilts in the bottom of the wagon, snug against the chill of Christmas Eve 1859. All of the Gossetts' belongings were piled high behind them, where Mary Tom, older than the twins by eleven months, leaned against a sack of flour. Pa Gossett sat in the driver's seat, face etched with the heavy responsibility of a widowed father, occasionally urging the family mule forward.

"This is our first Christmas without Ma," Rose choked. "I don't hardly see how we can stand it."

"Hush, Rose," Mary ordered. "We'll get through it."

"Things are bound to be better when we get to Coleman County," Sam assured the others, whistling in the dark to cheer up his siblings.

He did not actually believe the move would improve their life because this was the Gossetts' fourth move along the frontier from Fort Bexar and nothing ever changed. Pa suffered from that common pioneer itch to move on whenever a place became settled, always seeking greener pastures and more open spaces. Sam sighed, remembering how often Pa used to tell Ma that frontier homes were easy to break up and almost as easy to build somewhere else.

"Before long we'll be inside Fort Croghan and safe," Pa promised as he scanned the trail ahead. "Lucky for us that feller we met on the trail warned us about Indians nearby."

Moments later the winter dusk was pierced by scattered lights, announcing that they had indeed arrived at the safety of the fort. Soon they were strolling through the settlement, admiring Christmas decorations glimpsed through uncurtained windows. The children stared at fresh-cut cedar trees with bases wrapped in colorful, hand-pieced quilts. Most were festooned with strings of cranberries and popcorn, but a few boasted paper cutouts fashioned in snowflake designs. Still others flaunted colored paper chains with links stuck together with flour and water paste.

"Lookie there at that one!" Young Jimmy was jumping up and down and pointing to a tree towering in the window of a cabin attached to the blacksmith's shop. Constructed from twisted pieces of metal decorated with bolts, screws, and small tools, it was the strangest Christmas tree the Gossetts had ever seen.

Just as the family were heading back to their wagon to stir up a make-do supper, the door of a small cabin opened to reveal a slender girl with almost albino coloring. Shining, taffy-colored hair hung to her waist, and the backlight from the fireplace inside created the illusion of a halo. Sam would not have been surprised to see wings folded behind her shoulders.

"Children, vill you come in and have some cookies?" the vision invited in an accent that spoke of German ancestry. "You, also, sir," she added, turning to Pa and smiling.

"Thank you, ma'am." Pa nodded and the children jostled each other to see who could be the first inside. "I'm Ben Gossett, and these here are my younguns."

Once inside, Sam saw that this Christmas angel was nothing more than a very attractive girl who appeared to be about the age of his sister, Mary Tom. Her unusual height enhanced by the heels of her lace-up boots brought her almost eye to eye with Sam. Wide blue eyes above rosy cheeks and a generous mouth marked her as the prettiest girl he had ever seen, and he could not take his eyes off her. As he reached across for one of the cookies she was offering the children, his hand accidentally brushed against the bodice of her drab calico dress. Sam snatched back his hand and felt the heat of a blush rising across his face.

"I'm Gretel Hauser," their hostess informed the Gossets. Then turning to the children, she asked, "Where's your mother?"

"She died six months ago," Sam stammered.

"I'm so sorry." Gretel's eyes shone with sudden tears. "I know how sad you must feel. I lost my husband in September after we'd been married just two months."

"What happened?" Some of the tired lines in Pa's face seemed to soften as he eyed Gretel.

"We think his horse must have been spooked by a snake and pitched him to the ground. A rattler bit him, and by the time he was found he was dead."

"Do you have kinfolks here at the fort?" Pa inquired.

"Nobody here or any place else. I'm all alone in the world." Gretel glanced around her home and sighed. "Soon I won't even have this roof over my head. The man who owns the cabin is coming back to live here, and I don't know where I'll go. I hope I can find some family that needs help to take me in and give me bed and board in exchange for work. I can cook and sew and milk and do farm work."

Pa's eyes appraised Gretel as if he were contemplating buying a horse. "Would you consider going with us? We could be married whenever a preacher rides our way. This family sure needs a woman, and you seem to need a home."

For a moment Sam was speechless. Then his face flamed as he exploded, "Pa! She's young enough to be your daughter!"

"I'm already fifteen." Gretel smiled and let her eyes wander over Pa from head to toe. "There's no men hereabouts under sixty without a wife. You're a right fine looking man, Ben Gossett, and not more'n forty I'd guess. I'll think on your proposal."

Pa grinned. "Take your time. Just give me an answer by day after tomorrow when we'll be heading out to Coleman County."

Six months passed, and the Gossetts had settled in a rough-hewn cabin on the bank of Hords Creek. In the distance rose the gentle slope of Robinson's Peak, and behind the cabin a small herd of longhorns grazed among the prickly pears beneath mesquite trees with thorny tentacles that lashed out at Pa and Sam when they rode too close. The landscape was in stark contrast to the remembered beauty of Bexar County but held a peculiar charm all its own.

In the side yard a wooden windmill flapped in the breeze above an iron pump, and several hens and a red rooster pecked at the ground beneath. Inside the adjacent chicken coop a proud hen announced her daily contribution of an egg. Twenty yards to the right old Bess, the milk cow, lay tethered to a stake outside the barn chewing her cud. On the other side of the cabin a well-worn path led through the underbrush to the two-hole outhouse.

The June day seemed perfect for a wedding as four people eagerly awaited the upcoming ceremony. Ben and Gretel had looked forward to the arrival of the preacher for months to legitimize their union. After solemnly pledging themselves to each other, they were already living together as man and wife--not the first frontier couple to "jump the broomstick" while waiting for a saddlebags preacher covering vast areas of scattered settlements to ride their way to perform an official ceremony.

The Reverend William Robinson was seldom home on his ranch in the area, more often far from home riding the outposts of the frontier. When news spread that Brother Robinson would soon reach their community, Mary had insisted on making it a double ceremony. She was already promised to young Matt Thompson, and neither she nor Matt wanted to chance how long it might be before the preacher came their way again.

While Sam had accepted the substitute ceremony between Pa and Gretel as binding, the thought of them together continually consumed him with resentment and unacknowledged jealousy. Now that Gretel had assumed the role of stepmother, Sam tried to push his attraction to her into the darkest corner of his mind. Only in the sleepless hours before dawn did he admit that he wished it were he instead of Pa with Gretel in the curtained alcove that served as their bedroom. Jealousy was a sorry bedfellow as he lay on his pallet beside his siblings in the main room of the cabin.

When Gretel, pale and listless, had begun to have difficulty keeping her breakfast down, Sam was sickened by the thought of Pa making another baby. How could he after Ma died trying to birth that premature mite who survived her by only a few hours?

Sam fought his attraction by nourishing resentment of Gretel, seizing on her old-country ways and speech patterns as irritants. He kept comparing them unfavorably to the plantation manners and musical drawl of his Southern mother with voice as soft as Alabama cotton. In an effort to force Gretel's bouts with nausea and her coils of straw-colored hair wound atop her head to blot out the memory of his angel of Fort Croghan and the spell cast by her sky-blue eyes, he became deliberately surly and rude to his stepmother.

So it was that at the appointed time for the ceremonies when Gretel asked Sam to fetch Mary and Rose, he glared at her and growled, "You're not my ma! You can't tell me what to do." As tall as she was, Sam looked down on Gretel from a towering height that promised to rival that of the Texas hero whose name he bore.

She looked up at him and sighed. "I'm only asking you to do what your Pa told me to."

"Oh, all right," Sam conceded. "I'll round up the girls."

His frown melted into a grin as he thought of the young man who would soon be his brother-in-law. Matt Thompson, tall, tan, and lean with rusty brown hair flowing to his shoulders, at twenty-three already owned his own spread and enjoyed some success as a stockman. Sam aimed to be just like him in a few years and was glad Pa approved the match. Gretel also urged the match, making no secret that she thought it was time for Mary to marry and move out, leaving one less mouth to feed.

Sam found the bride-to-be playing a childish game with her sister.

Like Ma before her, Mary barely topped five feet, but her figure with its rounded hips and swelling bosom proclaimed her womanhood. When Sam found the sisters, they were in childish mode, giggling and jumping from a high bank into the sandy bed of the creek, careless of their Sunday print calico dresses.

"Lucky for you the creek's low and that sand's dry," Sam remarked. "It's wedding time. You better hurry," he urged. "The preacher's here and the family and neighbors are waiting to see you hitched."

The girls stood up, brushed the sand from their skirts, and smoothed their hair. "Race you!" Mary challenged.

Sam sprinted behind the girls, then caught up with Mary. He laid his hand on her arm, forcing her to pause. "You ain't getting' married just because you feel in the way, are you?"

"Course not. I love Matt and want to spend the rest of my life with him." Mary smoothed back the glossy brown curls that resulted from sleeping the night before with her hair rolled on rags. Then she lowered a fringe of long, dark lashes over one dancing blue eye in an exaggerated wink. "Besides, I can't stand the thought of being a old maid!"

"Not much chance of that," Sam laughed, "even if Matt wasn't around."

The trio walked the rest of the way until they reached the gathering in the yard. There Sam and Rose hung back to greet the Williams family, the Gossetts' closest neighbors. From a vantage point behind the ample bulk of Mr. Williams Sam eyed the dyed-in-the-wool Baptist preacher. The Reverend William Robinson stood tall, with skin darkened to hickory from a lifetime outdoors and grizzled beard flowing below his collar. Above high cheekbones, hawk's eyes bored right through to the very soul of anyone who met his gaze.

Robinson spoke sharply to two dusty hounds that had followed him on the trail. "Down, Moses! Stay, Joshua!"

Sam approached the preacher and asked, "Why do you travel with your dogs?"

"Haven't you heard, son? I take 'em along with me to tree

Campbellites so I can preach to them," he chuckled.

Sam retreated to a spot beside Rose and whispered, "He looks more like an outlaw than a preacher. Can't you just picture him shutting up those rowdies in Hazel Dell who were disturbing his sermon by declaring he was there to preach the Gospel by the grace of God and his trusty rifle?"

"Ain't you glad he's just passing through on the way to that revival over at Deer Crossing?" Rose whispered back to Sam from behind her hand. "If he stayed here till Sunday, we might have to sit through one of his famous four-hours-at-a-whack sermons."

Sam struggled to subdue a grin and continued to whisper. "Pa says that man's as full of wind as a cyclone headed for the barn and would argue doctrine with Jesus Christ his self."

Rose studied the preacher's face. "Give him his due. No trail is too dangerous or cabin too remote for him to be on hand for a baptism, marriage, funeral, or revival. He's sure dedicated to saving souls."

The twins continued to watch Robinson as he walked to his mule, removed from the saddlebag his deerskin-covered *New Testament* and *Book of Psalms*, faced his audience, and began to pray.

The ceremonies stretched on and on as Robinson quoted scripture after scripture and admonished the couples of their duties to each other. Finally he pronounced both couples duly married, and Gretel served kuchen and cider.

As soon as the preacher and guests had departed, Matt loaded Rose's pine chest filled with her meager belongings into his wagon and took his bride by the hand. "Time to go, Mrs. Thompson. It's a long ride to the ranch. As it is, we'll have to camp overnight somewhere."

Rose clung to Mary, fighting back tears. "I hate to see you go."

Mary returned her sister's hug and whispered, "Rose, come visit soon. I'm afraid I'll be mighty lonesome with no other women on the ranch."

Mary stepped back from Rose and hugged the whole family, each in turn. Then with a boost from Matt she climbed to the wagon seat and waved goodbye to her home and her childhood.

Sam kept an eye on his twin as she went inside the cabin. Moments later he was surprised to see Rose storm outside, stamp her foot, then pick up a rock and hurl it down the trail as she moaned, "I can't believe it--Mary took Lady Rebecca!"

Sam avoided reminding his twin that the doll actually belonged to Mary, who had generously allowed Rose to play with her. Lady Rebecca was a pretty piece of work as frontier dolls went, carved for Mary by Uncle Tump with arms and legs that moved on pegs and a dress Ma had made from flour sacking dyed with tea leaves. Sam recalled the many happy hours both sisters had spent playing with the doll.

"I know you think Mary ought to of outgrown dolls, her being a married lady now."

"Why couldn't she of left Lady Rebecca for me?" Rose sobbed.

"Mary's going off to a new life in a strange place. Maybe she just needed something to remind her of home," Sam mused. "Rose, how about you and me go down to the barn and sit a spell?"

"What for?" Rose rubbed tears from her eyes and looked up at Sam.

"Wouldn't it be nice to talk about happier times and how things used to be before Ma died?"

Rose nodded, and soon they were sitting in the hay, sifting through their combined recollection of earlier days. She was the first to unravel the tapestry of common memories.

"The first thing I remember is Pa running the ferry across the San Antonio River. Remember when somebody would shout 'B. J. Gossett, bring over the boat!,' one of us would run fetch Pa."

"We sure had some wild rides on that old ferry and that cottonwood canoe Pa made," Sam chuckled.

"Remember playing in the shade of the Alamo and pretending to be Davy Crockett and Jim Bowie?" Rose gestured as though firing a rifle.

Sam grinned at the picture in his mind. "Afterward we'd hide out of sight and watch the Injuns, whites, and Mexicans kick up dust along the streets of Fort Bexar."

"How their spurs jangled and guitar strings twanged!" Rose remembered. "Did you ever know how scared I was when a cowboy laughed too loud or cracked off a shot from his pistol?"

"No, you put up a good front and had me fooled. What I remember best is how I loved to hear Pa's stories about the fall of the Alamo and the massacre at Goliad and how the Texans got even at San Jacinto. How proud Pa was that he was there at San Jacinto with Houston when he captured old Santy Ana."

"Ma had her share of stories, too. Her favorite was about the Runaway Scrape and the women and children leaving their homes and traveling to the Brazos to escape the Mexican army."

"I treasure all the stories," Sam acknowledged. "I also remember how every time Pa decided to move on we had to pack the wagon and hitch up the oxen and hit the trail. I was always mad cause he'd never let me drive the wagon."

"Poor Ma had to ride horseback, pregnant or not, and drive the hogs ahead of her. Me and Mary sure got sick of listening to squawking chickens tied in cages at the back of the wagon and tending smelly younguns. We had many an argument about whose turn it was to clean up a stinky baby. At least you got to ride herd on the livestock."

Later that night Sam tossed back and forth on his pallet, tormented by dreams of men and women together: Pa and Gretel, himself and Gretel, Matt and Mary.

Autumn chased summer away, and Sam became more and more restless. Then on a cold night forecasting winter Gretel gave birth to a lusty son christened Englebert and fondly called Bertie. Sam resented the boy from the moment of his birth and faulted Pa for allowing Gretel to select his name instead of giving him the name of a Texas hero like all the other Gossett sons. Sam avoided both Gretel and the infant, refusing in his mind to accept him as a brother. However, the coddling and attention lavished on the new arrival more than made up for Sam's lack of enthusiasm, adding fuel to the fire of his resentment.

Chapter 2
THE RUNAWAYS

Early in the spring of 1861 the Gossetts received the following note from Mary: "Things are fine here on the ranch. Matt stays busy with the stock, and I have a hard time keeping up with the cooking and laundry for the hands, specially now that I'm expecting a baby. I could sure use some help. Can the twins come for a visit? Rose, I so long to see you. There are no women near here." Pa made no comment on the invitation, and the twins dared not ask if they could go.

However, a few weeks after Mary's letter arrived Sam took Rose aside and told her, "I got to get out of here. You must know how I feel. Ma always said twins have a special bond."

"I know." Rose nodded and placed a hand on his shoulder. "You think we're just in the way here and Mary needs us, so why don't we go stay with her and Matt?"

"Exactly what I was thinking. You can always read my mind." Sam frowned. "Pa won't give us permission, but I bet Gretel would be glad to get shut of us." Sam saw Pa in his mind's eye, shoulders stooped by hard labor, agate blue eyes hard, face weathered by years of Texas sun, and knew in his heart that Pa needed him here. On the other hand, he rationalized, Pa might appreciate the temporary relief Gretel would have with two fewer mouths to feed and care for.

Rose took Sam's hand, and mischief sparkled in her eyes. "Why ask Pa? Let's just leave a note and go. The Williams family is leaving Friday, moving on beyond Matt's place, and I'm thinking if we just show up and tell them we want to visit our sister they won't say no to giving us a ride in their wagon."

"Let's do it!" Sam exclaimed. "We can fix us some grub for the trail and sneak out before daylight."

Thursday night after everyone else was asleep, the twins lighted a candle and packed their clothes in a battered carpetbag, along with a few treasured and well-worn books. They shared Pa's love of reading. Although he had never attended formal school more than a few months at a time, he had devoured every book he could lay hands on: Dickens, Thackeray, Darwin, and the Bible. The twins had their own small library consisting of *The Iliad*, *David Copperfield*, *Jane Eyre*, and *Wuthering Heights*, dog-eared volumes passed on by transient settlers in exchange for a little sugar or flour or bacon.

Pa had seen to it that his children attended school whenever available. Where there were no schools, they soaked up knowledge from any literate adults encountered along the way. The end result was that Mary and Rose and Sam could read, write, and do sums with skill disproportionate to their time spent in the classroom.

On Friday long before the first streaks of dawn fingered the eastern sky, the runaways were dressed and eager to leave. Sam had the pocket watch left him by his grandfather wrapped carefully in oiled paper to protect it from moisture, and Rose wore her mother's gold locket. Even though she treasured her legacy, she had once confided to Sam that she would really have preferred the brooch that went to Mary.

The twins tiptoed toward the cabin door, pausing just long enough for Rose to lay on the kitchen table a folded note addressed to Pa. It read simply, "Gone to visit Mary if we can get a ride with the Williams family," and was signed "Sam and Rose."

"You're welcome to ride with us as far as Matt's," Mr. Williams assured them later. "Nice you can visit your sister."

Mrs. Williams smiled at them. "I do declare you two are cookie cutter twins. Same chestnut hair, same blue eyes, same face. Except Sam's taller and Rose prettier, I'd be hard pressed to tell you apart!" she giggled.

It was slow going for the oxen yoked to the heavy wagon, and early darkness overtook the travelers long before they reached Matt's ranch. When a lighted window told them they were near Cousin Grace Gossett's cabin, they sought shelter for the night. Mr. Williams announced that he and the Missus and the boys would just snug into the barn, and Cousin Grace welcomed the twins into the cabin.

"It's still a mite chilly inside. You can bed down on pallets in front of the fire. I'm sure glad of your company. My men folk are off hunting, and it gets powerful lonesome at night."

After their long, tiring day the twins were soon fast asleep until they awoke toward morning to the thud, thud, thud of heavy footfalls on the roof. Scattered embers were barely glowing in the fireplace as both jumped up, shivering .

"I'm the only man around here, and I don't mind telling you, Rose, I'm scared," Sam admitted.

Just then Grace came out of the bedroom, cool as spring water, dingy flour-sack nightgown billowing around ample bosom and hips. "It's that cussed painter again. No other critter in these parts is that heavy."

"What'll we do?" Rose quavered.

"Quick!" Grace barked orders like a drill sergeant. "Poke up the fire, and make sure the shutters are latched."

"They are," Sam declared as he checked to make sure.

"Then we're safe?" Rose swallowed hard., and Sam knew she was remembering her close call a few years ago when he had shot a panther sleeping in the sun on a limb overhanging the path she had just taken on her way to the spring for water.

"Not as safe as I'd like." Grace stared at the still dying embers in the fireplace. "That varmint could drop down the chimney."

Sam raced to Grace's bed, threw back the covers, and grabbed a corner of the straw-filled mattress, motioning the women to do likewise. Together they dragged the mattress into the fireplace, and quick as a hummingbird Grace poked the embers until the mattress was ablaze. The stench of burning straw filled their nostrils, and they began to cough as some of the smoke billowing up the chimney wafted back into their faces.

"That should discourage our prowler," Grace assured the twins. Soon a muffled thud outside the window told them the panther had leaped to the ground.

Sam peeked through the shutter in time to see the panther running away. "There he goes. The son-of-a-gun's the biggest painter I ever saw."

Nobody slept much after that, and at first light the twins were back in the Williams' wagon ready to hit the trail. The sun was high in the Eastern sky when the travelers reached Turtle Creek and began to ford the stream. Halfway across, a wheel dropped off the edge of a rock ledge, and the clumsy wagon tipped on its side like a cow stepping in a prairie dog hole. Household goods scattered in all directions, sending up showers of glistening spray, and everyone in the wagon tumbled waist deep into the stream.

"Gawd Almighty," Mr. Williams bellowed. "What a mess!"

Mrs. Williams and Rose scrambled to recover the cages of squawking chickens barely afloat, and Sam waded toward the Williams menfolk to help them set the wagon upright. Then began the task of salvaging and reloading wet quilts, bags of flour and sugar, pots and pans. Water dripped from the drawers of an oak dresser, and a tin washtub floated beside the wagon.

"Reckon any of this stuff will be usable?" Sam asked.

Mr. Williams shrugged and shook his bald head. "Hard to tell till it dries out."

More trouble lay ahead. The opposite bank of the creek proved too steep for the oxen, straining forward at the crack of Mr. Williams' whip as he waded next to them. The wagon refused to budge until Sam and the Williams boys put their shoulders to the rear boards and shoved with all their might.

"That's got it" Mr. Williams whooped as the wagon inched its way behind the oxen up the steep incline.

"What a day!" Sam muttered to Rose as he climbed up beside her where she perched on the back of the wagon, wringing out her skirt. "I feel like we earned our ride just now."

Finally near sundown the travelers arrived at Matt's ranch without further mishap. The sisters hugged and cried a little. Then Rose lit into Mary, and Sam saw she was spoiling for a fight.

"Where's Lady Rebecca? Why'd you kidnap her?"

"I never!" Mary glared at Rose. "She belongs to me. I just let you play with her all those years. Now she's put up for my little girl."

"I hope you have all boys!" Rose taunted.

Arguments were a way of life with the Gossetts. Tempers would flare and harsh words fly. Then afterwards things would settle down and go back to normal. So it was with the quarrel over Lady Rebecca. Sharp words were forgotten as Mary battled nausea and fatigue and Rose shouldered most of her chores. Sam was proud of his twin for carding and spinning, weaving and knitting, cooking over the open fireplace, sweeping the packed dirt floor with a broom made of broom weeds. He tried to ease her burden by giving her a hand with milking, churning, and digging in the garden.

The only time Rose complained was when wash day rolled around. "Nobody knows how I hate wash day. If you didn't help me with it, Sam, I'd never get through it."

Every wash day Sam patiently followed her instructions. "Build a fire under the wash pot and keep it hot. Then fill the pot about three-fourths full of water."

Once the fire was going under the pot, it was, "Now while we wait for it to boil, I'll cut up the lye soap into the pot. Please God let there be enough soap to last till we go home. I don't want any truck with making soap."

When the water started to boil, Rose would put the white items in the pot and punch them up and down for fifteen minutes to loosen the dirt. Then she would lift them out with the punching stick, let the water drip back into the pot, and beat them against the battling board to remove the water. Next the clothes would go into a pot of clean water to begin the rinsing process.

"Sam fetch more water from the well. It takes two tubs of clean water for rinsing. As soon as the second rinse is ready, I'll put the white wash in it. Then I'll give the colored dresses and shirts a quick dip in the suds and put 'em in the first rinse water."

Last would come a pile of filthy overalls and work clothes for all the men. "Sam, please put these in the boiling suds while I finish rinsing the whites and colored dresses and shirts. They'll probably need several trips back and forth between the battling board and the suds."

Once everything was clean, Sam would watch Rose spread the wet laundry on porch rails, bushes, and weeds to dry, taking care to place colored garments in the shade if possible. He would think of Gretel doing the washing back home and wonder who was helping her now that he and Rose were gone.

"Sam, thanks heaps." Rose would always give him a little hug. "Go on with your own chores now, but help me keep an eye out for the clothes while they're drying. Can't have all these clean things ruined by high winds or stock or yard dogs or barn cats."

Etched in Sam's memory was that first wash day evening when he had taken Rose aside after supper. "You look mighty tuckered out, Twin."

"I'm at my row's end and ache in muscles I didn't even know I had," Rose had complained. "After the clothes dried, I had to heat up that old flatiron on the stove and iron them. That thing must weigh as much as a heifer!"

Sam had rubbed her shoulders, advising "Get to bed early, and Ill do the same. Chopping wood and hauling water for your wash has plumb wore me out."

Chapter 3
CATTLE AND COWBOYS

Week followed week with relentless repetition of the same chores until Sam began to long for something more manly than helping Rose. Then one day Matt told him, "It's time you started riding the range."

Matt gave Sam a horse, a lariat, a pistol, and a rifle; and Sam was proud that he needed no instruction in handling them. He had grown up roping and riding and was no stranger to pistol and rifle. As far back as he could remember, he could fire a rifle even when he was so small he had to rest the barrel on a stump. Food for the Gossett table had often depended on his hunting skill.

Out on the range with herds of different owners mingling together without benefit of fences Sam observed first hand the difficulty of keeping stock separate. Instances of unintentional branding mistakes were common, and identifying mavericks was complicated by wranglers short on scruples and handy with a branding iron. Once Sam was privy to an incident when even the preacher was accused on this score.

It happened one day when he was searching for strays beyond the boundary of Matt's ranch that he spotted Brother Robinson in conversation with the widow McCracken at her watering trough. Knowing that the wiry, short woman with flaming red hair straggling beneath her flowered sun bonnet was a staunch Methodist, Sam suspected the contentious Baptist preacher would follow his usual custom of provoking a doctrinal argument. So he dismounted and stepped behind a large live oak to listen.

He watched Robinson take from his saddle bag the long-handled gourd he used for a drinking cup, dip some water, and sprinkle the head of his gray gelding.

"What in tarnation are you doing, Bill Robinson?" Mrs. McCracken demanded.

"I have as much Scriptural authority to sprinkle horses as Methodists have to sprinkle babies."

"Brother Robinson, everybody knows the River Jordan is so swift and has such steep banks it would've been impossible for John to duck Jesus," the Methodist argued.

"Then how long was the gourd handle John used to reach down from those steep banks to dip the water to sprinkle Him?" Robinson countered.

The widow shook her finger in the preacher's face and sputtered, "About as long as the handle of the branding iron you used to brand my stray bull yearling last week!" Robinson chuckled, mounted his horse, and rode away without another word nor a backward glance. I guess he couldn't top that, Sam thought.

Weeks later Sam was riding herd one night. The longhorns were milling and tossing their heads as the cowpokes exchanged uneasy glances. In the distance thunder rumbled and echoed on the heels of zigzag lightning that ripped the canopy of darkness at its outermost edge along the western horizon. Fingers of apprehension fluttered along Sam's spine as his eyes traveled beyond the brush edging the mesa to the steep cliffs that dropped into deep arroyos where a stampeding herd could plunge to a cruel death.

As the storm advanced, branched veins of electricity exploded into the ground at the very edge of the bawling herd. Thunder bellowed louder than the terrified cattle, and uneasiness weighed heavier on Sam's shoulders than his wet jacket soaking up the downpour falling from the storm-tossed clouds. Over the din of the cattle between thunder claps he heard the chief wrangler shout, "Turn 'em, boys! Quick before they head for the cliffs."

Sam spurred his horse forward to the very edge of the mesa only to find that he was the only rider able to reach the area ahead of the cattle. He swallowed the bitter taste of fear as thundering hooves and tossing horns bore down on him, closer and closer. Waving his hat, he whooped as loud as possible into the wind and fired his pistol in the air, certain that he would never see another birthday and that Matt's cattle would never reach market.

Sam prayed for a miracle and was rewarded. No more than two feet from his horse the foremost steers swerved and began to turn. Soon the cattle were milling in a circle, and the cowboys were able to drive them to a safe distance.

"Good work, boy!" The head wrangler tipped his hat to Sam. "Without you we'd have lost the whole herd." After that Sam rode just a little taller.

Back at the ranch, Sam never knew from day to day what to expect but welcomed the occasions when he was allowed to accompany Matt to outlying areas. On one such occasion they drove some cattle to Camp Colorado on Jim Ned Creek to provide beef for soldiers garrisoned there. While they were there, the Reverend William Robinson was scheduled to preach to the soldiers and some Choctaw Indians camped nearby. Sam was not inclined to endure one of Robinson's famous hour-upon-hour sermons, but Matt was curious to see the Indians' reaction; so they joined the audience.

Sam began to squirm as the sermon soared on and on. The Choctaws also grew restless. Finally, one by one, they rose and filed out. Sam wished he could follow suit. At length the service ended, and Sam and Matt strolled though the camp and saw the garrison commander approach a Choctaw brave and ask, "What did you think of the sermon?"

"White man lie--him talk too long." With that, the Indian returned to his camp.

Sam and Matt agreed that the comment would have repercussions. "I'll bet from now on Robinson will be known as Choctaw Bill,"

Sam predicted. He was right.

When the travelers returned to the ranch, the girls rushed to meet them with words tumbling over each other. "We were so scared we nearly peed our drawers," Rose began. "All the men were down at the corral fixing a broken fence, and Indians rode up to the cabin."

"When we saw them coming," Mary added, "we hid under the bed and hoped they'd think there was nobody home. We peeked under the edge of the quilt and watched them file by and look through the shutters. I was terrified!"

"They spoke to each other, but we couldn't understand their lingo," Rose continued. They were probably saying 'Nobody home" because they went on and rode away."

"You were wise to stay out of sight," Matt told the girls. "You were probably safe enough with men working at the corral, but some Indians are still taking settlers captive."

Sam filled in details. "I heard at the fort about a small white child some Indians abandoned in a bed of giant cactus. On the way home we found two children wandering alone. A white boy and girl about ten, naked as Adam and Eve afore they ate that apple."

"They ran like wild mustangs when they saw us," Matt added, "but we managed to rope 'em. They couldn't speak a word of English. Guess they wuz captured by Indians as babies."

"What became of the poor things?" Mary asked.

"We took 'em into the nearest settlement and found them some clothes and families who would keep them as help around the place," Matt explained. "I sure don't envy those folks the job of trying to civilize that pair. I doubt they'll ever find out who they are or whether they're brother and sister or from different families."

Cowboys, being natural drifters, came and went from time to time. One day a muscular young man named Bryan Cookson drifted in and hired on as one of Matt's hands. He was capable enough, but something about his stocky figure and black hair slicked back and tied at the nape of his neck, together with his insolent manner, set Sam's teeth on edge. He had a feeling that something was not quite right about the newcomer, a suspicion that became full blown when he observed that the initials on Cookson's wallet and watch did not match his name.

One night when the other hands were out on the range, Sam found himself alone in the bunkhouse with Bryan. He put his arm around Sam and suggested, "Let's you and me have some fun while the others is gone."

Sam pulled free. "What do you mean?"

"What do you think I mean?" Bryan leered.

Sam stared at Bryan, turned on his heel, and strode from the bunkhouse, recalling stories he had heard of what sometimes went on in cow camps far from female companionship. He did not go back to the bunkhouse until some of the other men returned, and after that he was careful to stay clear of Cookson. He considered reporting the incident to Matt but thought just maybe Bryan's proposition was meant as a joke on a tenderfoot and giving it credence would hold him up to ridicule.

A few weeks later Sam noticed that Rose had begun to disappear just after supper for a little while each evening. After a time he confronted her as she left the cabin. "Where are you going, Rose?"

"For a walk before bedtime."

"Mind if I come along?"

She colored slightly, then muttered, "I'd rather you didn't."

A frisson of alarm nudged Sam to action. What was happening to the twin who always sought his company and shared her thoughts? He hung back until Rose was almost out of sight, then followed her at a distance until she neared a grove of cottonwood trees beyond the bunkhouse.

Keeping to the shadows, Sam crept forward just as Bryan Cookson stepped into view. He watched the pair murmur together in a manner suggesting a romantic tryst. Then the cowboy placed his hands behind Rose's neck, pulled her forward, and tried to kiss her. "No, you mustn't!" Rose jerked free and started to run away.

"Aw, come back, Rose." Bryan coaxed. "You're just so darned pretty I couldn't help myself."

Rose continued her way back toward the cabin without answering. Sam wanted to knock Bryan down and pummel him with his fists, but that could wait. Instead he followed Rose, overtook her, and grabbed her by the arm. "Rose Lucille Gossett, what do you think you're doing meeting that no-account Bryan Cookson?"

"None of your business." She pulled away from her brother.

"I'm making it my business."

"Now, Sam, don't get all riled up. He likes me, and I enjoy his company."

"You don't know him like I do. Take it from me, he's no good. You're sure to get hurt if you keep on seeing him."

"Mind your own beeswax." Rose stepped into the light shining from the cabin window, and Sam noticed that their mother's locket, which she always wore, was not around her neck.

"Where's your locket?"

Rose clutched at her throat. "I don't know, It must have dropped off somewhere. Maybe the clasp was loose."

The twins retraced their steps along the path to the cottonwood grove and searched high and low. The locket was nowhere to be found.

The next morning at sun-up Lefty came early from the bunkhouse and shouted to Matt, "That good for nothing Bryan Cookson pulled out in the night. He taken my silver spurs, Duke's nearly-new hat, and a few dollars from the rest of the boys."

"And Rose's gold locket!" Sam exploded, remembering how Bryan had reached around Rose's neck and pretended to try to kiss her.

Matt lost no time in rounding up a posse to ride after the fugitive and allowed Sam to come along. When they returned, Lefty was wearing his silver spurs. Sam handed Rose her locket without a word.

"What happened to Bryan?" she quavered.

"You don't want to know." Sam ran his forefinger across his throat.

Rose burst into tears. "Oh, Sam, I'm so ashamed that I let myself fall for his slick gab and fake compliments."

Sam scowled at his sister. "It's over. Forget it. Just see that your next beau is more suitable."

A few weeks later the twins were pulling weeds in the garden when they saw a stranger approaching at a leisurely canter. When he reached the yard, he flung himself from his roan mare and asked for Matt. Their resemblance was unmistakable. The tall, tan, lean young man with long, rusty brown hair might have been Matt five years earlier.

"You must be Matt's brother!" Sam exclaimed.

The stranger extended his hand. "Tim Thompson from Erath County."

Sam grasped his hand. "I'm Sam Gossett, Mary's brother. This here's my twin, Rose."

Tim turned his attention to Rose and broke into a wide grin. "I see I'm gonna like it here."

Just then Matt hurried from the direction of the barn and enfolded Tim in a bear hug. "Gosh, it's good to see you, little brother!"

"Thought I'd come for a visit, maybe stay awhile and give you a hand."

"Plenty of work and plenty of room in the bunkhouse," Matt assured Tim. "Stay as long as you like."

Chapter 4
THE OUTCAST

In the weeks that followed as Sam and Tim rode herd together, they became fast friends. When Tim began to show a marked interest in Rose, Sam was pleased. "I think Tim's sweet on you," he teased Rose one day.

She blushed. "I don't mind if he is."

"I wonder what Pa will say?" Sam mused.

As if on cue, Pa came riding in with eyes cold as steel. His jaws were clenched and his mouth set in a thin slash across his face. "I've come to fetch you runaways home. I'm willing to overlook you taking off without permission 'cause I know you wanted to help your sister. I would've been here sooner, but Gretel's been sickly with a new baby on the way and I couldn't leave."

"Not again!" Sam slammed his hand against the porch rail. "Gretel's no better than your brood mare or your hound bitch always ready to whelp." Sam allowed his true concern to surface. "You kept on breeding Ma till she died of it. I can't stand to see that happen to Gretel."

Pa drew back his arm and delivered a hard slap against the side of Sam's head. "Shut up! I'll have no more of your insolence. You've had a chip on your shoulder ever since me and Gretel got hitched. Babies are just a normal part of being married, and I won't stand here and listen to you speak of my wife like an animal."

Sam stood perfectly still except for the curling and uncurling of his fingers. His mouth was set in a hard line for all the world like Pa's, but he said not a word. His silence infuriated Pa still further. "I've put up with your mouth over the years, but this time you've crossed the line. You are no longer my son nor welcome in my home."

Pa clenched both fists and continued. "I'll thank Matt not to keep you on here either. From now on you're on your own." He turned to Rose. "I'll be leaving in the morning. We can talk later."

That night in the bunkhouse Sam lay awake and pondered what he could do and where he would go. Tempers often flared and as quickly cooled in the Gossett family, but Sam knew deep inside that this time Pa would not cool down nor budge from his ultimatum. Sam was still awake when the hands readied themselves for breakfast, silent on the subject of his banishment. Perhaps they did not yet know he would be leaving. As soon as everyone but Sam had exited the bunkhouse, Rose appeared in the doorway with biscuits and bacon and coffee.

"Sam, that big mouth of yours has got you in a heap of trouble. Better come back to the house with me and apologize to Pa."

"No. I can't go home and watch Gretel's belly getting bigger every day and think about Ma."

"It's your choice, Sam. Pa lashed out at you in a fit of temper because what you said to him was plumb awful. I don't understand what it is with you about Gretel, but I think he'd accept your apology and take you home. He's agreed since it's almost time for Mary's baby to be born I can stay till then. With a first baby, he thinks she needs me more than Gretel and says Polly Sue's plenty big to help till I get back."

Sam hung his head and examined his boots. "I won't apologize and go home, and I can't stay here. I don't know what I'll do."

"Maybe Matt has some ideas. He wants to see you and said for you to wait here till he comes."

After breakfast Matt strode into the bunkhouse and threw a packet on Sam's bunk. "I'm sorry about this mess you've brought on yourself, but you know I can't let you stay." He pointed to the package.

"Here's some flour and sugar, coffee and salt, jerky, a pan and a cup and matches. You can take the Appaloosa you been ridin', your rifle and pistol, rope and canteen. Best bet is to head south until you find some rancher that can use a extra hand. There should be wild game aplenty to keep you going."

Sam threw his arms around Matt's shoulders. "Thanks! I didn't know what I was gonna do. Now I know I can get by."

"Better spend another night here and get an early start tomorrow. I'll send Rose with something for your supper. Just stay out of your pa's way until he leaves."

"I'll leave at daybreak tomorrow. Tell Rose and Mary I'll get word to them somehow where I am."

As soon as the eastern sky was blushing with dawn's first kiss, Sam arose without waking anyone, dressed, and swallowed a biscuit left over from supper. He washed it down with a cup of cold coffee from beneath his bunk and tiptoed to the corral to saddle Patches. He inserted his packet of provisions in his saddle bag, strapped on the pistol and slung rifle, rope, and canteen over the saddle along with his bedroll containing his clothes. He looked around him at the cabin and the bunkhouse and fought back a single tear, vaulted into the saddle, and was off.

Careful to keep the rising sun to his left, he headed south to whatever the future held in store. He rode at a steady pace until the sun was high overhead, then stopped at a clear stream. After choking down some jerky with the aid of water from his canteen, he refilled the canteen and resumed his journey to nowhere.

As evening closed in, Sam found himself in the edge of a cedar brake dotted with an occasional live oak. He reined Patches to a halt and slid to the ground on legs weary from gripping the saddle. He tethered Patches and gathered enough wood for a small fire, then unrolled his blanket, picked up his rifle, and positioned himself several yards away from his campsite.

Before long a scrawny jackrabbit scurried into view. Sam took aim and fired, skinned his supper with his Bowie knife, and was soon sating his hunger with roasted rabbit. On his bedroll by the fire after supper he drifted into an uneasy sleep disturbed by the distant howls of coyotes. The next morning when he left the campsite to relieve himself, a deer bounded away at his approach and a flock of wild turkey took flight. He cursed himself for leaving his rifle behind and vowed henceforth to keep it always handy. Lesson number one in survival.

Sunburned and saddle sore, Sam continued southward. Day followed day in much the same pattern. Twice he came upon small ranches and stopped to seek work. Nobody needed another hand; so he kept riding on. One day, still seeking a haven, he found himself at a ford across a running stream and spurred Patches into the water. At the edge of the stream, Patches shied away from a water moccasin and catapulted Sam from his saddle head first against a huge rock. He seemed to be spinning around and around until he came to rest in a black void.

Sam had no idea how long he faded in and out of consciousness, shivering in his wet clothes. During one lucid interval he managed to pull himself ashore, grateful that the deadly moccasin had kept its distance and moved downstream. The last thing he remembered before sinking into a deep stupor was Patches standing beside him nuzzling his shoulder.

When Sam finally regained consciousness, a strange odor assailed his nostrils and he looked around to locate the source. A circular, slanting enclosure, rising to a a point overhead told him he was in a teepee. In the center of this lodging a pot of herbs simmered over a small fire, filling the air with a pungent medicinal odor. He tried to rise from his pallet of deerskins but fell back exhausted and realized he was very ill. He turned his head and focused on the buckskin-clad figure with black braids and copper skin seated cross-legged beside him.

"Where am I," Sam mumbled. "How long have I been here?"

"*Tres días*, three days. *Está Vd. en mi casa*, my home."

The stranger flashed Sam a smile, exposing even white teeth. He continued in two languages. "*Buenos días*. Good morning. *Bienvenido*, welcome. *Vd. muy enfermo*. You have been very sick."

"No comprendo Español." Sam managed the few words of Spanish in his vocabulary.

"Ah, then I speak English only."

"Who are you? How is it you speak two languages yet appear to be Indian?"

"Three languages, counting Choctaw. My brothers call me Running Wolf. I am *mestizo*, what you would call half-breed. My father was a Mexican caballero. He taught me Spanish and English. When he died I came to live with my mother's people. She was a Choctaw princess and taught me her language."

"I'm Sam Houston Gossett. Just call me Sam."

"You bear a noble name. *El presidente* of the Republic earned great respect, even from many Mexicans."

"My father fought with him at San Jacinto. I hope that doesn't offend you."

"Not at all. *Mi padre* joined the Texas forces and died at Goliad in the massacre."

"Thank you for saving my life and taking care of me. I guess I caught pneumonia lying in wet clothes until you found me."

"It was my daughter Singing Bird who found you. You had fallen and hurt your head and spoke much of running away. So we call you Fallen Runner. That is your Choctaw name while you are with us."

During Sam's slow recovery Singing Bird brought his food. He looked forward to the sight of her lithe figure and shiny black braids and the musical lilt of her soft, strangely-accented English. When at last he was strong enough, he joined Running Wolf and his companions in hunting, fishing, tanning hides, and playing games. Sam soon felt at home with the Choctaws and was content, remembering how his idol, Sam Houston, had run away from home in Tennessee in his early teens to live with neighboring Cherokees. He had even taken a Cherokee bride named Tiana. Yet he had succeeded in becoming Governor of Tennesee, Commander-in-Chief of the Texas armies, President of the Republic, Governor of Texas, and a U.S. senator.

A number of suns and moons after his rescue Sam came to

Running Wolf. "The time has come for my sister Mary's baby to be born. She and Rose must be sick with worry over me. I promised to get word to them where I am."

"Then, Fallen Runner, you must go."

"I'll leave at daybreak and return as soon as I have seen my sisters."

After three days of hard riding Sam found himself once again on Matt's land and was seized by dread that Matt would turn him away. In his eagerness to see Rose and Mary he had stopped only long enough to eat, to rest Patches, and to refresh himself with a few hours of sleep. As he neared the cabin, he saw cowhands working near the corral and Rose doing the washing in the side yard. Relief washed over him as he observed that Matt was nowhere in sight.

Sam rode into the yard and whistled. Rose looked up, shaded her eyes with her hand, then ran toward him.

"Sam! Sam! Is that really you?"

He leaped from Patches, grabbed her, and swung her off her feet, then stepped back to appraise the change in his twin.

"Why, Rose, in the short time I've been gone you're all growed up and filled out. Bet fellers come from miles around to court you!"

Rose blushed. "Sam, I'm so glad you got here today. I'm going back home in the morning with neighbors headed that way."

"How's Tim?"

"He took up some land near here and started a herd. He rides over to see us often."

"To see you, you mean?"

"I guess so. He keeps talking about us getting married."

"Have you said yes?"

Rose smiled. "Well, I haven't said no."

Sam looked around. "Where's Matt?"

"He left this morning to join some Rangers at Hords Creek."

"Is there trouble?" Sam asked.

"Not really. Some Tonkawas pitched their camp at the water hole near the settlement and the Ranger camp, and Choctaw Bill converted and baptized many of them. They often came into the settlement and embarrassed the women who lived there."

"What did they do?"

"Half-naked braves would walk into settlers' cabins without knocking and sit around the fireplace to watch the bread baking. They'd lift the lid of the oven and poke their dirty fingers into the soft dough to see if it was done. This didn't set well with the cooks."

"Were the Rangers able to do anything about that?" Sam asked Rose.

"Yes. They told the Indians the sins washed off by baptism in the water hole where they drank had entered some of their babies and made them sick! The whole tribe pulled up stakes and moved further down the creek away from the settlement. The Rangers just want to be sure they stay there."

"Can I see the baby?" Sam looked toward the cabin. "Tell me about him."

Rose giggled. "For starters, he's a she. Her name is Sammy Rose, and she's the prettiest little thing you ever saw."

Just then Mary appeared in the cabin doorway, saw Sam, and ran to embrace him. Tears wet her cheeks. "You're a sight for sore eyes, Sam. We were afraid we'd never see you again. Come inside and see our Sammy Rose."

"That's why I come!"

Mary laughed. "You can spend the night. Matt won't be home, and we won't tell. I want to hear all about where you've been."

Later Sam sat at the kitchen table with his sisters and wolfed down fried chicken, biscuits, and gravy while telling them about his accident and how Running Wolf and Singing Bird had nursed him back to health.

"Life with the Indians is good," he assured his siblings, "but I'm hungry for news of what's happening across the state. Is there still talk of war?"

"It's way beyond talk," Mary told him. "Texas seceded from the Union in spite of all Governor Houston could do to prevent it. He did everything except take Lincoln's offer to send Federal troops."

Rose chimed in, "General Sam was thrown out of office because he wouldn't take the oath to support the Confederacy. Edward Clark, his lieutenant governor, is now Governor of Texas."

"A lot's happened since I left," Sam commented.

Mary's face betrayed her anxiety. "Now that Texas is part of the Confederacy, a lot of men have rushed into military service. Thank God, so far Matt and Tim are content to serve in the Texas Rangers and will probably stay here on the frontier instead of joining the Confederate troops."

Rose sighed. "That's dangerous enough."

"Enough about the war." Sam changed the subject. "Tell me about yourselves."

Rose frowned at her sister and shook her head, then gave in. "Oh, all right, Mary. Tell on me like you always do."

Mary's eyes twinkled, and a broad grin split her face. "Sam this twin of yours has gone and disgraced herself! Tell him about it, Rose."

"Out with it, Rose Lucille Gossett!" Sam demanded.

"You know how much we always hated to be told we couldn't do this or do that or we'd be turned out of church. If you'd a been here, you'd have gone along with me."

Sam smiled. "Which Baptist commandment have you broken? Drinking? Card playing? What?"

Rose laughed. "None of those. I went to a dance in Campbell Corners with Tim. He's a Campbellite, you know."

"Well, I never! What was it like?" Sam prodded.

"Glorious! There was a fiddler playing and a caller telling us what steps to do. Couples were skipping and swinging their partners. I soon caught on and was dancing to do si do, allemande left, then right and left grand. Everybody was laughing and having a good time, and I didn't see the devil chasing any of us. It was great fun."

Mary interrupted. "The very next Sunday the local Baptist congregation turned Rose out of church."

"How'd Pa take that?"

Rose turned pale. "He don't know yet."

"I guess the news'll get to him soon enough. I'm glad I won't be here when he finds out!" Sam patted Rose's shoulder.

Finally he asked the question uppermost in his mind. "How's Gretel?"

"Sad and depressed," Mary told him. "She lost the baby. Then little Bertie died of a fever. She hasn't been herself since."

"Dear God!" Sam exclaimed. "Poor Gretel."

That night, once again in a real home, Sam thought of his teepee and realized there was no place for him here. He longed to comfort Gretel but knew he could not go home. He must honor his promise to Running Wolf and return to the Choctaw village.

The next morning as Sam was lifting Rose's carpetbag into the neighbors' wagon, Mary came out and handed her Lady Rebecca.

"Here, Rose, you take her. I have Sammy Rose now."

Sam had forgotten the dispute over the doll. He thought that neither sister needed a doll any more now that both had grown past childhood.

Rose wrapped Lady Rebecca in her shawl and said, "Thank you, Mary."

"I'm the one should be thanking you for all the help you've been. I don't know what I'd have done without you." Mary hugged Rose tight.

Rose looked at Sam. "I'll just be a minute. I'm going back inside for one last peek at our namesake."

"I'll go with you." Sam turned and followed her.

Inside the cabin the twins tiptoed close to the cradle, and each placed a kiss on the sleeping infant. Then as they turned to go, Rose unwrapped the doll from her shawl and laid her in the crib beside Sammy Rose. Sam nodded his approval, and together they went out to the waiting wagon.

As Rose headed home, Sam waved good-bye, then saddled Patches and took the trail leading back to the Choctaws.

Chapter 5
INDIAN BRIDE

On the return journey Sam allowed Patches an easier pace and stopped more often to enjoy the April splendor of the landscape. Clumps of low stalks waving bright blue blossoms like miniature sunbonnets blanketed the meadows. Scatters of red Indian paintbrush, orange and yellow fire wheel, pink primrose, purple verbena, and little yellow daisies rested like fragments of fallen rainbows among the billows of bluebonnets.

Squirrel and wild turkey were plentiful and fresh water readily available. At night he lay by his campfire and studied the stars. The howl of distant coyotes no longer disturbed his slumber. He knew he could trust the fire to keep them at bay. Instead, dreams of Gretel and Pa caused him to toss restlessly, and he awoke wrestling with an urge to go home and try to make his peace with Pa.

One star-studded night on his way back to the Choctaw village Sam was startled to see three riders gallop into the glow from his campfire and yank their horses to a standstill. He reached for his pistol, but the tallest of the three spurred forward and knocked the weapon aside.

"No need for that. We're in charge here," the man bellowed. His voice put Sam in mind of a bull yearling.

As the man's two companions raised their rifles, Sam eyed the red-bearded stranger and asked, "Who in tarnation are you?"

"Name's Red, and I'm the boss of this outfit."

He pointed to each of his companions in turn as they dismounted. One was a short, stocky man with leathery skin and a patch over one eye. The other was a skinny black man with the trigger and middle fingers missing from his left hand.

"This here's One-eyed Jack, and that's Three-finger Joe."

Sam recognized two of the horses the strangers rode as mounts belonging to his Choctaw friends. "Where'd you get those horses, and what do you want?"

"I reckon you can herd cattle, can't you?" Red asked.

"What's it to you?"

"We need you. Choctaws killed old Pete what was riding with us and left us short a wrangler to drive our herd to Colorado."

Sam had no doubt some of the cattle, like the horses, were from the Choctaw village. "Can't help you. I'm headed south."

"Not now you ain't," Red growled. "Yer going with us to Colorado."

"How you goin'ta make me herd your cattle?"

"Easy. We take your grub, your weapons, your bedroll, and your horse," One-eyed Jack explained.

"You won't last long afoot without food or guns." Three-finger Joe grinned, exposing white teeth stained with tobacco juice.

"If I go with you, then what?" Sam asked.

"We'll let you ride your horse," Red told him, "eat your grub, and sleep on your bedroll."

"Guess I got no choice," Sam muttered. "What happens when we get to Colorado?"

"We'll cut you loose and you can go where you want to," Red promised.

In order to survive, Sam fell into the routine of riding herd on the stolen cattle, several marked with brands familiar to him. The rustlers kept his feet tied together underneath his horse and watched him constantly. Even if he managed to escape, he had little hope of returning to his friends without food, water, and a weapon. He clung to the hope that the Choctaws would be following their stolen livestock.

On the third night Sam sat at the campfire eating squirrel stew. When he finished he lay down on his bedroll upwind from One-eyed Jack and Three finger Joe, who had obviously not bathed for a very long time. As usual his feet were hobbled, and his hands had been tied behind his back. After his captors were asleep and he had drifted into uneasy slumber, he was startled into wakefulness by a faint rustling sound. At first he thought it was a breeze in the leaves of the surrounding trees, but when he opened his eyes no wind was stirring.

Suddenly shrill war cries pierced the silence of the night as dark figures swooped down on the camp and bound Sam and his captors. Sam recognized his Choctaw friends, but they seemed not to notice that he was hobbled and already a prisoner. The Indians herded their prisoners closer to the fire, and Running Wolf recognized Sam.

"Fallen Runner! Why are you riding with thieves?"

"I'm their prisoner. They forced me to go along to survive after they took my food and weapons."

"Now I see." Running Wolf swiftly unbound Sam. "We wondered why you were so long in returning."

"Thank you, my friend. This is the second time you have rescued me!"

"I'm glad we found you. Now to take care of these *bandidos*."

"Turn 'em over to the Rangers. They'll see they get a fair trial, then hang."

"Their fate is a decision for our council, not your Rangers."

"Running Wolf, how can I ever repay you?"

"There is a way."

"Anything you ask."

"It is Singing Bird. She has come into her womanhood and refuses to accept Black Hawk as her husband although they have long been promised. She is free to do as she pleases because she is the daughter of a princess."

"I'll speak to her if you think it will do any good."

"It will do no good, Fallen Runner. She has made up her mind that she will have no husband but you. Will you take her?"

Sam experienced a feeling of déjà vu. Sam Houston had his Cherokee wife; now would his namesake marry Singing Bird? He thought of the slender maiden who had nursed him through illness. The doe eyes and black braids were in stark contrast to the blue eyes and blonde mane that haunted his memory, but the Indian maid stirred a longing deep in his loins.

"I will do as you ask, Running Wolf. I'll take Singing Bird with your blessing and be a good husband to her."

After they returned to the village, Singing Bird donned ceremonial feathers and was married to Sam according to Choctaw custom. The people of the village chanted and danced in celebration, all except Black Hawk. Afterward the newly joined couple retired to a teepee spread with deerskins and bright woven blankets to explore the joys of manhood and womanhood.

She lay beside him, trembling and murmuring, "Do I please you, Fallen Runner?"

"More than I dreamed possible. Please call me Sam. You are now Mrs. Sam Gossett."

In the months that followed, Sam and Singing Bird took great pleasure in each other's company. Sam was glad Running Wolf had taught his daughter English and pleased to find her vocabulary growing as he recounted stories of his childhood, his estrangement from his father, life on Matt's ranch, and anecdotes about Choctaw Bill.

Singing Bird was especially attentive when he told her stories from the Bible about creation, Moses and the Ten Commandments, David and Goliath, Daniel in the lion's den, Jesus and His miracles, His death and His resurrection.

One day she said, "Sam, Singing Bird want to be Christian, to be baptized and married by real preacher. Would your Choctaw Bill do that?"

"Yes, he would. He has converted and baptized hundreds, maybe thousands, of people from the Rio Grande to the Red River, whites and Indians alike. His travels take him in many directions far away from his ranch and home. It could be many months before he rides this way."

"When he comes, then I be one of your people." Sam did not have the heart to tell her that neither baptism nor marriage would make her one of his people nor that the white community would always see her as an outsider of inferior status. How could he explain that the Christian love-thy-neighbor teachings he had quoted to her did not extend to Indians?

Singing Bird longed and waited for Choctaw Bill to come baptize her and perform a Christian marriage ceremony, but he did not ride their way. With each passing sun and moon, Sam came to love his Indian bride more. All but forgotten were the blue eyes and blonde locks of his stepmother, which had led to his banishment from home. Brown eyes, copper skin, and gentle ways caused him to think less and less often of his white family. He began to feel as though he had always been part of the Choctaw village, and thoughts of returning to the white world as Sam Houston had done faded. His life was here.

Some months after their union Singing Bird told Sam she was with child. "Now us a real family. Me very happy, Sam."

Sam had misgivings about becoming a father until he remembered something Pa had once said about having babies being a normal part of being married. Before long he was as excited as Singing Bird about the baby. A pang of conscience told him that this had been how Pa felt each time Ma or Gretel became pregnant, and thoughts of Pa cast a shadow over his happiness. The only place for a mixed-breed child would be with the Indians. He could never take Singing Bird and the baby home, and Pa would never know this grandchild.

Three months before her time, Singing Bird came to Sam with sorrowful eyes. "The baby comes too soon. I am much afraid." They sought out Quanoma, wise in the ways of birthing. The older woman's face was a map of fifty winters of biting cold and as many summers of brutal sun. She helped Singing Bird into her teepee and ministered to her while Sam paced the paths of the village and waited. Finally Quanoma emerged and spoke softly to Running Wolf, who stood motionless outside the teepee. Then she raised her voice in a high-pitched wail, which was soon taken up by the other women of the village.

Sam grabbed Running Wolf by the shoulders. "What does it mean?"

"The child does not live. The women are mourning."

"I must go to Singing Bird and comfort her."

Running Wolf placed a hand on Sam's arm. "Quanoma says she is very weak and barely clings to life."

Sam wrung his hands in an age-old gesture. "What can we do? She's too young to die."

"Nothing can be done. The bleeding continues too long." Running Wolf dropped his gaze earthward to hide the pain in his eyes.

"I must see her," Sam insisted.

"Go and say *adiós*."

Inside the teepee, Sam tiptoed to the pallet covered with deeply stained deerskins and took Singing Bird's hand in his. "Don't leave me."

"I must, Sam. I will be with our son."

"No! There has to be something I can do."

"One thing, Sam," she whispered. "Bury me Christian."

"I promise," Sam choked as her lifeless fingers slipped from his. "Good-bye, my little Singing Bird. Fly away to a better place."

Later while Sam dug a tiny grave for the son who would never be and Running Wolf prepared that of the mother, Sam kept trying to remember the right words for a funeral service. As if guided by angels to this spot, at this very moment Choctaw Bill Robinson rode up on his mule followed by his two hounds. He dismounted and fixed his keen gaze upon Sam, naked above the waist, burned as dark as an Indian, with long hair in braids.

"Sam Gossett, I scarcely knew you. You are much changed since last I saw you."

"Brother Robinson." Sam spoke in a voice husky with emotion. "My wife Singing Bird has waited a long time for baptism and a real marriage ceremony. Now it's too late, but I beg you to grant her last request for a Christian burial."

After counseling with Sam, the preacher gathered the Indians together and stood beside the fresh graves.

"According to Sam here, our departed sister has declared herself to be a Christian and requested baptism."

He stood in thought for several minutes, then came to a decision.

"I can't baptize her in a stream as is my custom, and I refuse to sprinkle like the Methodists. But I hereby declare that Singing Bird is baptized in the Spirit and joined in Christian matrimony to Sam Houston Gossett."

Sam grasped Robinson's hand and let tears flow unashamed. "Thank you. She would be so happy."

Robinson sermonized, briefly for him, for an hour and a half about Jesus and His promise of eternal life, then closed with a prayer. Singing Bird's last request had been granted, her wishes fulfilled.

Afterwards the preacher drew Sam aside and spoke privately with him. "Sam, I'm afraid I have bad news about your pa."

"Don't tell me he's dead, too!" Sam's blue eyes probed Robinson's face for the answer.

"No, not dead--but maybe worse. He had a stroke and is helpless. Part paralyzed and unable to move his legs."

"Who's managing the ranch?"

"Gretel--as best she can," Robinson answered. "She's got a lot on her plate what with the younguns and tending your pa."

"What about Mary and Rose?"

"Mary's expecting again. Rose married Tim and they have a baby on the way."

"A lot's happened since I've been gone. Jim and Polly must be growing up and big enough to be considerable help."

"They do what they can, Sam, but they need you. It's time to go home."

"I want to, but part of me is here and I doubt I can patch things up with Pa."

Sam turned to Running Wolf for counsel. "What should I do?"

"Fallen Runner, it is for you to decide. I think your heart tells you one thing, your pride another. It is never a mistake to follow your heart."

Robinson's hawk eyes bored into Sam's blue ones. "The frontier's a hard mistress. Necessity often dictates action. Your pa married Gretel to keep the family together. She ain't your ma, but she does her best. Your pa and the children have come to love her."

"I believe that."

"I don't know what passed between you and your pa. He never told me, but he needs you now."

"After the ugly, hurtful words we spoke, I don't know if he'd want me to come home. I'll have to think on it."

"Pray on it," Robinson advised. With that he mounted his mule ready to set out on his next mission.

Before prodding the beast into motion, he turned and eyed Sam. "I'll be coming by your Pa's ranch in a month or two. I expect to see you there."

Sam slept fitfully that night and awoke at dawn, resolved that come what might he must go home. He embraced Running Wolf. "*Adiós, amigo*. You have been a good friend, and I have found much happiness with your people, as well as sadness. Now I must go home." He mounted Patches.

"We will miss you, Fallen Runner. *Vaya con dios*." Running Wolf smiled. "I see you are traveling Indian style in your moccasins."

"My boots are no longer comfortable."

Chapter 6
NEW IDENTITY

For two days Sam kept to the trail without incident. Then on the third morning he awoke to a dull yellow sky and an uneasy feeling that the air around him had become heavier. Scattered rain beat down upon him from time to time. By late afternoon he kept glancing over his shoulder at the threatening sky until his fears became reality. There on the horizon appeared what Texans with an eye on the weather dreaded most. A black cloud dipped earthward, took on the unmistakable shape of a funnel, and began to spin like a top. Sam's mouth went dry at sight of the twister, and he longed for the old storm cellar at home.

He looked on all sides for a creek bed, ditch, or depression in the earth sufficient to protect him from the fury of the wind. Staying in the open or beneath a tree would be fatal. He spurred Patches forward at a gallop in an effort to outpace the storm until he spied a shallow crevice some three feet deep. It was not enough protection for the appaloosa but hopefully enough for a man's body stretched full length at the bottom.

Sam dropped from the saddle, sent Patches on his way with a slap from the flat of his hand against the rump, and dived into the meager shelter. The full force of the wind bore down on him out of control. He buried his head in his arms, lay flat, waited, and prayed. As a boy he had once stood near the tracks as a freight train roared past and could have sworn a train was bearing down on him now had he not known how remote this area was from any rail lines.

Sticks and stones, birds, and a jackrabbit whirled overhead in the vortex of the storm, then rained down on Sam, spewed from the maw of the cyclone. As the roar of the storm passed beyond him, he ventured to raise his head and glance beyond his shelter. Two dozen yards away, he saw Patches swirling high above the ground, borne aloft by the maelstrom of wind. He rose to his knees and retched.

When he finally deemed it safe to stand, he examined himself and found only superficial cuts and bruises. The scene surrounding his safe haven resembled a war zone. Giant trees were twisted and uprooted. One tiny branch was driven straight through a large limb. A hawk was impaled on the horns of a dead buck. Patches dangled across the limb of a century-old oak ten feet above the ground, neighing piteously. The unfortunate beast's left foreleg hung twisted and broken as the appaloosa struggled feebly.

Sam picked his way through fragments of disaster, soothing his faithful mount in a calm voice that belied his inner turmoil. Tears coursed down his cheeks as he spoke to Patches, "Good-bye, old friend and faithful companion. I'll miss you."

He drew his pistol, took careful aim, and fired. As Patches stopped struggling, Sam holstered his pistol and wiped the tears from his face with his bandanna. Then he climbed the oak until he reached the place where Patches rested. He stroked the motionless head and collected his rifle and ammunition, canteen and meager supplies, rolling everything in his blanket. Carefully he levered it from limb to limb as he backed down the tree away from the dead horse and useless saddle. At the foot of the tree he sat down and wept.

The trail he had been following was no longer distinguishable. Could he make it home on foot with nothing to guide him? Chances were slim, but he was alive and uninjured. As far as he could see, the countryside was littered with detritus from the twister. Sam was forced into a macabre dance of constantly sidestepping rocks and tree limbs and soon found that his moccasins, fine on a trail, were no match for the rough terrain he was traversing.

The next day he reached a wide expanse of hilly countryside untouched by the tornado and knew he had completely lost his way. Nothing looked familiar. He was footsore and thirsty and carefully rationing the water in his canteen until he could find a stream to replenish it. To exacerbate his misery, a dense cloud of reddish brown dust hung above the dry plains to the west and was headed in his direction.

Before long the wind was whipping cruelly at his face, driving grit into his eyes and nostrils. He began to choke and cough and tied his bandanna over his nose and mouth as he plodded onward with head bowed. Soon layers of blowing dirt obliterated the sun and reduced visibility to zero. Several times Sam stumbled and fell, but recovered his footing and pressed doggedly onward toward an unknown destination.

Then without warning he stubbed his toe against a stump and plummeted headlong into space. When he touched the ground, he tumbled over and over, torn by cactus and bruised by boulders. While he rolled downward, he clung to his rifle and supplies as if to a lifeline. As his body jolted to a stop, his head struck a large rock at the bottom of the ravine. Then blackness.

When Sam regained consciousness, he sat up with his head throbbing and no memory of what had happened nor that this was the second head injury he had sustained. He saw that his clothes were covered with dust and a bandanna still covered his face although the atmosphere was clear. How long since he had been in a dust storm and fallen? Where was he? Who was he? Where was his horse?

Sam gathered up an empty canteen, a rifle, and assorted supplies that he supposed were his. Then he surveyed his surroundings. A line of cottonwoods snaked along the bottom of the ravine below him, and he knew without knowing how he knew that trees spelled water. Soon he was filling his canteen from the trickle running along the creek bed and scooping up handfuls of water to drink and splash over his face and head.

Sam was perplexed that he could function normally yet could not remember his name. He knew how to locate water and use rifle and pistol. He tested his memory by reciting multiplication tables and spelling words. He sang a few bars of "Come to the Bower" and whistled a mockingbird call. Everything in his memory seemed to be in place except who he was and where he had been.

While he wondered about his identity, Sam searched the pockets of his buckskin pants for a clue. He pulled out his grandfather's watch with crystal smashed and hands stopped and read the faint inscription "To Jeff from Lucy." Thinking that his name must be Jeff, he let the puzzle of his past rest and realized that he was hungry. He shot a rabbit and built a fire. Then he cooked the rabbit and ate half of it, saving the remainder for later. After satisfying his hunger he began to walk with no idea of where he was going.

The next day he picked up a trail that brought him to the edge of a tiny settlement with the name QUAIL RUN crudely lettered on a board nailed to a post at the side of the rutted dirt road. On the main street a handful of weathered buildings huddled along plank walks covered with a layer of dust. A giant of a man with grizzled hair and beard stood in front of the general store stirring the dust with a worn broom. At sight of a stranger he propped his broom against the wall and strode into the street to meet him.

"Who are you?" he demanded. "What do'ya want here?"

Jeff, as Sam now supposed himself to be, looked around him and saw a red and white striped pole that spelled barber shop.

"My name's Barber, Jeff Barber. Lost my way and wandered here. I need to find work to pay my keep."

The big man looked Jeff over and, apparently satisfied, extended his hand.

"Larry Hines. This here's my store, and I reckon I could use some help. Last feller moved on. You kin sleep in back, and my wife at the Busy Bee Cafe across the street will give you meals. Beyond that, I can't pay nothing."

"Bed and meals will do just fine for now," Jeff assured Hines, relieved that his immediate needs had been so easily met.

Three weeks later Jeff was arranging sacks and cans in the storeroom behind the main store when the bell on the front door jangled to announce a customer. Larry was minding the store; so there was no need for Jeff to go up front.

Out of sight, but well within earshot, Jeff heard Larry ask, "What kin I do for you, stranger?"

"You kin give me all your cash," a rough voice snarled, "and some coffee, flour, and sugar, or I'll blow you to kingdom come."

"No need to get riled, stranger." Larry's usual brusque voice took on a soothing tone.

The stranger guffawed at that. "Don't you know who I am?"

"Can't say as I do."

"The Coleman Kid, that's who! Don't you read the posters in the sheriff's office? I've killed ten men tougher'n you. This time I'll just tie you up. Then I'm gonna hit the bank."

There was nothing Jeff could do here but keep out of sight, but maybe he could warn the bank. Careful not to make a sound, he grabbed a coil of rope and slipped out the back door. Then he crossed the street to the weathered frame building partitioned into two sections to accommodate both the barber shop and the bank. He glanced back at the store and saw that the outlaw's back was still to the street. He seized his chance, opened the door to the bank, and rushed inside.

"Mr. Binkley," Jeff warned, "the Coleman Kid's robbing the store and headed your way."

Binkley's eyes widened behind small, round, wire-rimmed glasses. "I can't stop him. Ain't drawn a gun in years. Nobody ever bothered the bank here in Quail Run before. There ain't that much money."

"You got a rug in your office?" Jeff asked.

"Yep, an old piece of carpet in front of my desk."

"Quick, help me drag it in here," Jeff urged.

Between them, they positioned the carpet crosswise just inside the front door. Then Jeff crouched at one end of it behind a coat rack that screened him from view from outside the window.

"Just stand behind the teller's cage and pretend to be counting money," Jeff told Binkley.

After a short wait, the door flew open and the Coleman Kid stepped inside. Jeff gave the rug a mighty yank, and the outlaw went sprawling on the floor. Before he could recover, Jeff jumped him and jammed his pistol against the Kid's ribs.

"Put your hands over your head!" Jeff ordered.

Then he turned to the banker. "Take his guns, and tie him up with that rope I brought."

Once the Kid was secured, Jeff marched him to the empty, unmanned jail and locked him inside its single cell. Alerted by Binkley, a half dozen curious men had gathered, all staring at Jeff.

"Where's the sheriff?" Jeff asked the townspeople. "Don't believe I've seen him since I got into town."

"That's cause we ain't got one," Binkley explained.

Larry Hines, whom Binkley had freed from his bonds, stepped inside the jail and removed something from the drawer of the desk. Then he pinned the badge with a star on Jeff.

"Here's our new sheriff! Agreed, fellers?"

"Agreed!" they chorused.

"Jeff," Larry told him, "you can continue our arrangement at the store and come over to the sheriff's office when you need to."

"A small salary goes with the job," the banker added.

"Good. First thing I'm gonna do is buy me some boots. Then I'll start being your sheriff."

The barber clasped Jeff on the shoulder and said, "I doubt you'll have much trouble with anybody once word gets out you captured the Coleman Kid. I expect there's a reward out for him that you can collect."

"I don't want more trouble, but I could sure use the reward."

Jeff continued to keep close watch on his prisoner until the Rangers came to pick him up and take him away for trial. After that the next few months were uneventful until the day the Indian rode into town.

From inside the store Jeff watched him leap off and tie his buckskin to the hitching post. When he entered the store, Jeff was instantly alert for possible trouble. No matter how well behaved the redskin might be, there were people in Quail Run who thought the only good Indian was a dead Indian.

Once inside, the Indian raised his hand in greeting to Jeff and spoke in the language of the Choctaws. "Fallen Runner, how is it you are here? We thought you had gone home."

Jeff was perplexed that he understood the Choctaw and amazed that he found himself answering in the man's native tongue.

"I got separated from my horse somehow and lost my way in a dust storm. Then I couldn't remember what had happened or who I was. Do you know me? Who am I?"

Before the Indian could reply, a crazed settler named Steve Sullivan stumbled into the store and fired two shots at close range. When the victim crumpled to the floor, Sullivan began to beat upon the lifeless body with both fists, tears streaming down his cheeks.

"Bastard savages. They killed my wife and stole my children. I'll never rest until I get them all."

"Simmer down, old timer." Jeff pulled the distraught man to his feet. "Who elected you this Indian's judge, jury, and executioner? There's no evidence he was guilty of the crime against your family."

"He's an Indian--that's crime enough," the old man sobbed. "They all got to pay."

"Damn you!" Jeff exploded. "He was about to tell me something important." Now he would never know what the stranger could have told him about his identity.

Jeff studied the dead Indian's face for some glimmer of recognition, but his memory remained locked. Only questions, no answers, swirled in his head. How did the man know him? Where had he been before he lost his memory? How could he understand and speak in the Indian's native tongue? Why had he been wearing moccasins, not boots, when he fell? Had he had a horse? If so, what happened to it?

Jeff looked at the aged shooter, sobbing piteously and obviously unhinged by his tragedy. What good would arresting him do? He would never be convicted of murder. White men killed Indians with impunity with far less provocation.

Jeff was so disgusted with frontier justice that he had no desire to spend another day as sheriff. So he crossed the street to the empty sheriff's office and threw his badge on the desk. Next he selected a saddle from the store, figuring the pay due him as sheriff would cover the cost. He saddled the Indian's buckskin gelding and untied him, then jumped astride, and galloped out of Quail Run without a word to anyone or a single glance backward.

He had come so close to information about his identity only to have the chance snatched away by a crazy old man.

Chapter 7
THE LAZY HAWK

Jeff resigned himself to living out his days as Jeff Barber and rode aimlessly onward until nightfall, discouraged, weary and hungry. He was looking for a campsite when he glimpsed a faint light ahead over the next rise.

As he rode nearer to this welcome sign of human habitation, Jeff saw that the light came from the single window of a shack carelessly clinging to the base of a low hill. Leaving his horse hitched to a mesquite tree, he walked to the cabin door and knocked.

"Who's there?" demanded a gruff voice from within. "Put yer hands up and show yourself at the winder."

Jeff did as instructed and assured the unseen occupant of the cabin, "I mean no harm. My name's Jeff Barber, and I been riding most of the day without food. Could you spare a cup of coffee and a biscuit?"

A red-bearded dwarf of a man with twinkling brown eyes threw open the door and stood looking up at Jeff.

"Come in, young feller, and I'll rustle you up some grub." He extended a stubby, callused hand to Jeff and added, "I'm Shorty Barnes, and this here's a line camp for the Lazy Hawk Ranch. Don't get much company this late in the day."

"I'd be much obliged for that grub." Jeff shook hands with his host and was met with a vice-like grip surprising in a man of such short stature.

Later after wolfing down a plate of beans and bacon, Jeff relaxed in front of the fire with coffee in a tin cup and warmed to his genial host. Unexpectedly, he found himself confiding the problem of his lost identity. Shorty listened with interest, now and then posing a question.

"You don't remember nothing before coming to with your head against a rock?"

"That's about the size of it. I can remember how to do everything that comes to hand. I find I can ride and rope and shoot and do sums and read. I just don't know who I am, how old I am, or where I come from before I took the name Jeff Barber in Quail Run."

"That knock on the head must of done it to you," Shorty surmised. "Best thing you can do is quit worrying about the past and be happy being Jeff Barber. Maybe some day you'll remember everything."

"I've about given up hope, but I long to go home."

Shorty put his hand on Jeff's shoulder. "Curl up there by the fire and get some shuteye. Tomorrow I'll send you to talk to the owner about a job here on the ranch. Think you kin handle it?"

"Bet I can. What kind of man is the owner of the Lazy Hawk?"

Shorty chuckled and slapped his thigh. "Bless me, didn't I tell you? The owner's a woman. Miz Sophie Hawkins. She's a real young widder woman with a 8-year old son. A hard but fair-minded boss. The boys all respect her and will do anything for her, same as for Cal Hawkins when he was alive."

"I just hope she can use me. Got no place else to go." Jeff's face showed his concern.

"No need to tell her about your mem'ry if you don't want to," Shorty advised.

"For now, I think I'll keep it just between us."

At sunrise the next morning Jeff listened carefully to Shorty's instructions before setting out for the Lazy Hawk headquarters at a brisk canter. An hour later he reined in the buckskin and surveyed the scene fanned out before him. On the right sprawled a barn, a stable, and a bunkhouse; on the far left stood a small building that must be the kitchen. Adjacent to it a large, rectangular garden plot was green with bushes and vines. Sam recognized tomatoes, string beans, squash, okra, and watermelon. A few yards away a windmill turned vigorously in the breeze, pumping water into a pipe that drained into the garden.

The centerpiece of the scene, set in a grove of cedars and poplars, was a square, two-story frame house weathered to a dark gray. Wide porches bordered the front and sides of both stories and sheltered a scattering of wicker chairs and settees. As Sam approached the house, a woman opened the screen door and shaded her eyes with her hand to study him. Elbowing her aside, a sturdy, brown-haired boy dressed like a cowboy burst through the door and pulled up short at sight of a stranger.

Jeff jumped from his horse and introduced himself, adding "I spent last night with Shorty. He sent me."

"I'm Sophie Hawkins." The young woman extended her hand and gripped his firmly. "This hellion is my son, Cal, Jr."

Jeff eyed the slender figure dressed in working pants, shirt, and boots with admiration. Shorty had neglected to tell him that the owner of the Lazy Hawk was beautiful. Her sun-kissed face, brown eyes and cloud of dark hair hanging in two long braids stirred a momentary response in Jeff's lost memory. Where had he known another slender maiden with brown eyes and black hair in braids? Why did the boy standing beside her trigger an instant of sadness for something lost?

The moment passed, and Jeff was explaining to Sophie Hawkins that he needed a job. "I'd be much obliged if you can use me."

"Any ranching experience?" she inquired.

"Yes, ma'am," he promised confidently although he could not remember any. "I used to work for my uncle," he fibbed.

Sophie Hawkins did not hesitate. "Then I guess we can use another hand around here."

"Does that mean I'm hired?"

"On a trial basis."

The boss of the Lazy Hawk turned to her son. "Cal, take Jeff down to the bunkhouse and see that he has whatever he needs."

Jeff mounted and swung the boy up behind him. "I have my own pony," Cal protested. "He's over in the stable."

When they reached the bunkhouse, Jeff looked around uncertainly. "Guess I'll just wait here until the foreman tells me what to do."

"You won't see Randy Boggs afore night," Cal told Jeff. "He's out checking one of the line camps. Stow your gear and come with me."

Jeff hid a smile at the easy way this young sprout had of giving orders. "Yes, sir," he answered.

Together they led the buckskin to the stable. Jeff unsaddled him and rubbed him down, then watered and fed him. He noticed that Cal was still hanging around.

"What's your horse's name?" the boy asked.

Jeff realized that a name had been the farthest thing from his mind since he had fled from Quail Run on the dead Indian's pony. He considered for an instant the circumstance by which he had acquired the mount and smiled.

"I call him Chance."

"Funny name for a horse. Why'd you name him that?"

"So little boys like you could ask me why. That's why."

"You got any kids?" Cal was full of questions.

"Nope." Jeff wondered if that were true. How could he really know?

"Do you think my mama's pretty?"

"Yes, I do." The thought of Sophie Hawkins standing on her front porch warmed Jeff's thoughts and stirred some vagrant memory.

"Will you marry her and be my papa?" Anxious brown eyes revealed the depth of his longing for his lost father.

"Thank you for asking, but I can't do that. Your mother and I scarcely know each other. I can't be your father, but I tell you what--I can be like a big brother if you want." Jeff wondered if perhaps he had a brother somewhere.

A grin spread across Cal's face. "I'd really like that. Can we start right now?"

"You bet." Jeff reached out and tousled the boy's hair, wishing he really were the boy's brother.

In the days that followed Cal was Jeff's constant shadow everywhere around the ranch headquarters. Jeff had it on good authority from the cook that whenever he was out on the range, the boy moped around the bunkhouse, the barn, and the stable.

One day Cal was watching Jeff saddle up when his mother walked into the stable.

"Mama, why can't I ride with the cowboys?"

"Because you're the man of the house and I need you here."

As the boy stalked off in a huff, Jeff turned to his boss. "I hope Cal doesn't take this man of the house business seriously enough to strike out on his own."

"I don't think he'd go far," Sophie Hawkins assured him.

Two weeks later she came to realize just how wrong she was. When Jeff rode in from mending fences, Boggs told him that Cal had disappeared. "He slipped away while Miz Sophie was going over the books in her office. His pony ain't in the stable. The kid probably rode out to watch some of the hands branding in the west pasture," Boggs guessed. "I sent one of the boys out to bring him back."

When the man returned without finding Cal, Jeff suspected that he might have a clue to the boy's destination. He remembered Cal's repeated tales about Caverna Maravillosa and his keen interest in the hidden gold reputed to have been hidden there by early Spanish explorers. Supposedly the cave stretched beneath the hills somewhere in the western reaches of the Hawkins pasture land. Cal had once shown Jeff a crude map with the cave marked by an X, but Jeff had dismissed it as the work of the eight-year-old's active imagination and paid little heed to the drawing.

"Anybody know where there's a cave somewhere on the ranch?" Jeff asked Boggs. "I think the boy may be trying to find it."

Boggs shrugged and looked around at the men gathered in the yard. All of them shook their heads.

"I've heard tell there is such a cave," Boggs told Jeff, "but I ain't got no notion of where it is. The story goes that the entrance is hid and you could ride right by it and never see it."

"I'll see if Miz Sophie knows about it," Jeff said.

He walked over to the house and asked, but she was no help.

"When I first came here, my husband told me the tale of Caverna Maravillosa, but I don't think he'd ever been there. I thought it was just a myth. I can't imagine where Cal got the map you say he showed you."

"Is there anyone who might know? I have a strong hunch that's where the boy has gone."

"If anybody knows anything about the cave, it would be Shorty Barnes. He's been in these parts longer than anybody else."

"Ma'am, with your permission I'd like to ride to the line shack and talk to him," Jeff offered.

"Go, and please hurry." Sophie's forehead was wrinkled with worry and her eyes bright with unshed tears. "Caves can be very dangerous, and Cal may be hurt."

Jeff saw that she believed in the cave. "Soon as I pick up a few things from the barn, I'm on my way."

Jeff took a lantern, some rope, an extra canteen, and a couple of blankets and set off at a gallop for Shorty's line shack. When he arrived, Shorty grasped both of the younger man's hands in his callused paws.

"How you doin', young feller?" he boomed. "Got your mem'ry back yet?"

"No such luck," Jeff answered, "though I did have a brief flash of someone's face that Miz Sophie reminded me of."

"Give it more time." Shorty placed a hand on Jeff's shoulder. "What brings you out here?"

"It's young Cal. He's disappeared, and I hope you can help me find him."

"What kin I do?" Shorty asked.

"I hope you can tell me about Caverna Maravillosa. I think that may be where Cal's gone. He showed me some kind of a map once. I never paid much attention. Thought it was just childish foolishness--buried treasure and such. Miz Sophie says if there is such a place, you may know where it is."

"So that's where my map went!" Shorty slapped his thigh. "That little rascal! I showed it to him one time. Then a long time later I missed it but didn't make the connection. Jest thought is was misplaced."

"Do you remember how to get to the cave?"

"I saw it once when I was a young squirt. Trouble is the entrance is hidden. Without the map you'd just have to stumble on it."

"Try to remember," Jeff begged.

"No use searching at night. Sleep here." Shorty advised. "You can git an early start tomorrow. Meanwhile I'll set myself to remembering the map and draw it off for you."

"Cal's life may depend on you," Jeff told Shorty. "I'll turn in early and be off at first light."

The next morning by the time the edges of the eastern sky had begun to pale in the distance, Jeff had breakfasted and saddled Chance and was going over last-minute instructions from Shorty about the crude map he had sketched out. Satisfied that he knew the general area of the hidden cave, he mounted and set out in search of Cal.

The sun was warm on his shoulders when Jeff sighted the first landmark on the map, a saddle-shaped hill ringed by a dense growth of cypress. Assured that he was headed in the right direction, he cantered westward until he reached the next landmark on his map, an underground spring bubbling up to the surface of the pasture land. From this point he began to ride in tight circles searching for the entrance to the cave.

He rounded a cluster of tall boulders screening everything beyond from view and reined in sharply. There was Cal's small paint pony tied to a cedar. His pulse raced. Cal must be here! Jeff dismounted and tethered Chance, then began to search every cleft in the rocks for an opening into the cavern. Ten minutes later he spotted a narrow fissure at the base of a hill behind masses of rock and weeds. It was barely wide enough for a man to worm through, and it led downward into the earth.

Jeff retraced his steps to Chance and brought the lantern, rope, and canteen back to the entrance of the cave. Thus prepared for whatever he might find, he wriggled through the opening and stepped out of sunshine into an eerie twilight. While there was still a faint light penetrating a few feet beyond the cave's entrance, he struck a match and lighted the lantern. Then watching each step because his life depended on it, he began to inch along the narrow path leading downward.

On both sides limestone stalagmites rose on tiptoe, and an occasional small grotto bubbled with crystal water. In places the path fell away in steep drops to unfathomable depths. Overhead, stalactites hung like gigantic icicles from the ceiling. Jeff felt that he had wandered into another world, a place of weird shapes and menacing shadows.

There was no sign of Cal, and Jeff's mouth was dry as he held the lantern out over each pit he passed and tried without success to penetrate its depth. From time to time he called out, "Cal! Cal!" The only answer was a hollow echo, "Cal! Cal!"

The path Jeff was following began to branch into openings on either side leading into other reaches of the cave. He saw that Caverna Maravillosa was a honeycomb of passages and chambers. Now that he knew Cal was here, he still might never find him. He thought of Sophie's pale, worried face and determined to keep trying. Could she, who had lost a husband, bear to lose a son? What if the boy were injured or dead, lying at the bottom of some pit?

Jeff moved forward on the assumption that young Cal had followed the main path, but he soon realized that he himself could easily become confused by the crisscrossing paths and lose his way back. So he took out his Bowie knife, cut off some pieces of rope, and unraveled the strands. Then he began to lay down a trail that he could follow back to the entrance.

At one point the path narrowed into a tunnel so low that Jeff was forced to stoop to get through. At the other end he found himself in a huge chamber of incredible formations as far as his feeble light could penetrate. Stalactites hung from the domed ceiling like pastel beaded draperies. Pillars of limestone protruded from the floor in a circus of shapes transformed by his imagination into a bear, a camel, a giraffe, and a lion.

He swept the lantern around him in arcs, holding the darkness at bay in first one corner, then another of the gigantic room. In one wall he saw a small alcove and moved toward it holding his light out before him. There huddled on the floor motionless was Cal.

He rushed to the boy and placed a hand on his shoulder. "Cal, it's Jeff. Can you hear me?"

The boy stirred and rubbed sleep from his eyes. "Jeff, I knew you'd find me! That's what big brothers do."

"Are you all right?" Jeff's voice broke with anxiety.

"I am now." Cal flung himself against Jeff and hugged him hard.

"How'd you get in here with no light?"

"I had a lantern, but I dropped it looking over into a deep hole. I brought lots of matches and used them all to find this spot. Then I sat down and waited for you to find me."

"Nobody knew where you had gone. That was very foolish to leave without telling anybody."

"I know," Cal sighed. "If I told, Mama would never have let me go."

"Nobody knew where to look for you until I remembered the map you showed me once."

"But you found me!" the boy protested.

"Cal, this is very serious. Do you realize you could have died here alone in the dark?"

The boy began to cry. Jeff wiped away his tears with his bandanna and said, "I know you want to go home. Stay close to me, and we'll get out of here."

As they followed the trail of rope strands Jeff had laid down, Cal began to laugh. "This is just like Hansel and Gretel and the bread crumbs!"

At the name Gretel, a page turned in Jeff's memory, and for just an instant he glimpsed rosy cheeks, blue eyes, and flaxen braids. Then the book of memory slammed shut.

"Jeff, I'm awful hungry."

"Didn't you bring anything to eat with you?"

"Yes, but I left it in my saddle bag."

"Then let's go get it. After you eat, we'll ride home and you'll have to face the music with your mother."

When Jeff and Cal rode into the stable at the Lazy Hawk, dusk had settled over the pastures. As they came across the porch, Sophie flung open the door and enfolded Cal in a hug that seemed to go on forever.

"I'm sorry, Mama. I won't never go off like that again." Cal promised.

"I ought to warm your britches," she scolded as she tousled his hair, "but I'm so happy to see you safe, I'll forgive you this time."

Sophie turned and gave Jeff a big hug, clinging to him a little longer than necessary and trembling. "How can I ever thank you?"

Jeff stepped back, his face red and his voice husky. "I'm just as glad as you to find him unharmed."

"I have an idea," Sophie told him. "Are you good with figures?"

"I think so," Jeff replied without really knowing for sure.

"I could use some help with the office work required to run this ranch," Sophie continued. "I'd like you to be my bookkeeper on a trial basis. If it works out, the job is yours permanently."

"What will the other hands think? They've all been here longer."

"They are good on the range and in the barn and the stables, but none of them have the gumption to handle ranch records. Nobody but you was smart enough to figure out where Cal had gone and how to find the cave."

"I was just lucky," Jeff protested.

"Maybe so, but I'm making you my assistant. Let the others think you got a promotion for finding Cal."

Jeff began spending one or two days each week in Miz Sophie's little office tucked beneath the stairs, learning how the ranch operated, where to order supplies, how to make entries in her ledger, and how to handle the payroll. Jeff's apprehension over his ability to do the job turned to pride when a month went by and there was not a single error in his figures. On the days that Miz Sophie did not need him in the office, he continued to work the ranch under the direction of

Randy Boggs.

While working so closely with Miz Sophie, Jeff found that he was developing feelings beyond the scope of an employer-employee relationship. Occasionally by accident her hand would brush against his as she pointed to an entry in the ledger or his knee would touch hers as he moved his chair closer to hers to examined an invoice. Other times she would place her hand upon his shoulder to get his attention when he was totting up figures and it was time for lunch.

Each innocent contact stirred in Jeff a longing for more closeness, and he read in Sophie's eyes that she felt the same. Inevitably a day came when, without quite knowing how, they found themselves in each other's arms. He was kissing her and stroking her hair, and she was kissing him back.

"Jeff, do I have to be the one to say it? I love you."

"And I love you, but there's something I have to tell you."

"Not now." She placed her forefinger against his lips, took him by the hand, and led him into the parlor.

"Jeff, say you'll marry me and help me run the Lazy Hawk forever. You know that Cal loves you, too, and would like nothing better than to have you for a father."

"Sophie, there's nothing I want more. I love you, but I can't marry you."

She drew back as though he had slapped her. "I should never have suggested it."

"Sophie, remember I told you there was something I must tell you? I can't marry you because I don't know who I am or whose name I can give you. For all I know, I could have a wife and children somewhere. I don't even know how old I am or where I come from."

Then he poured out the story of his lost identity and the watch inscribed to Jeff from Lucy.

"We'll not speak of this again until you get your memory back," Sophie's voice was husky.

"Your offer is a memory I'll treasure," Jeff promised.

"Maybe some day we can talk about it again. The time may come when you remember who you are, and we'll go on from there."

They returned to the office and to work side by side, day after day, keeping their distance. Jeff's feeling for Sophie filled him with torment, but as much as possible he avoided being alone with her. When he looked into her eyes, he saw his own distress mirrored there.

Chapter 8
SOLDIER OF FORTUNE

The year 1862 brought poverty and hardship to Texans everywhere. News spread even to isolated areas like the Lazy Hawk that Union warships were blockading Galveston harbor. It was nearly impossible to get sugar, coffee, and medicines. Flour and calico were very expensive. Clothing and shoes were scarce and had to be made at home by women or slaves.

Not being a cotton planter, Sophie kept no slaves. An old Mexican woman and her daughter did the cleaning and washing. Once, watching the young girl working at the wash tubs, Jeff had one of his transient memories. He glimpsed a chestnut-haired young Anglo woman washing clothes in the same manner; but the figure faded from memory, leaving the reality before him a dark-skinned Mexican girl.

Sophie worked hard to keep the ranch running and mend and make clothing for herself and Cal and the ranch hands. Leather was plentiful from cattle hides, and some of the wranglers were skilled at patching boots and shoes. Food was not a serious problem as there was plenty of garden produce, beef, hogs, and chickens to feed those at the Lazy Hawk. Often, however, there was no coffee nor sugar nor flour for bread and pastries.

The occasional traveler passing their way brought news of what was happening in other parts of the state. They learned that Texas had become the storehouse of food for the Confederacy because it was relatively free from Union soldiers. The penitentiary at Huntsville was manufacturing over a million yards of cotton cloth for use of the armies. An arsenal in Austin was manufacturing cannon from Mexican copper. A cap and cartridge factory was even operating in the chambers of the supreme court.

The blockade of Galveston continued, and the Union ships succeeded in keeping supplies out of Texas. By the end of the year the Lazy Hawk was in dire need of sugar and coffee and flour and medicines.

One day Sophie sent for Jeff and a towheaded young hand known as Cotton. "I want you two to take a few head of cattle to Austin and try to barter for some of the things we need so desperately."

The trip was successful, but Jeff was restless and sent Cotton back to the ranch alone with the supplies they had managed to secure. He realized something had to be done to open up the port of Galveston if Texans were to receive relief and decided to ride to Houston to see what was happening to lift the blockade. In Houston in January of 1863 he learned that General John Bankhead Magruder was in command of the Confederate forces planning to recapture Galveston. On impulse Jeff rode into military headquarters and offered his services.

"Can you use another fighter? I'm good with a rifle."

"You can start helping to haul artillery onto those two river steamers." A sergeant pointed to two vessels in the ship channel.

When the artillery was loaded, breastworks of cotton bales were put in place to protect the soldier-sailors slated for the mission to Galveston against four Union warships. Jeff stood with others behind a cotton bale with rifle ready when Magruder's odd fleet sailed down Buffalo Bayou and crossed the bay.

As the strange craft bearing Confederate marksmen moved across the quiet waters of the bay, the Confederate land force was passing over the bay on the railroad bridge. Soon the boom of artillery mingled with the chatter of rifle fire until together these forces captured or destroyed the Union ships blockading Galveston. Rebel yells pierced the air, and the port was once more in the hands of Texans.

After the blood and thunder of the battle Jeff had no stomach for further fighting. He was merely a temporary volunteer, not an enlisted nor conscripted soldier. So he made his way back to Houston, fetched Chance from the place he was stabled, and worked odd jobs for enough to pay for bed and board. Finally he started back to the Lazy Hawk. Because he was in no hurry to resume the stress of being close to Sophie, he took his time in a leisurely trek westward.

Farmers and ranchers along the way were glad to give him a bed and meals in exchange for a few days or few weeks of his help. He hung around the Capital in Austin a month getting the feel of conditions in other parts of the state. Then he rode toward Fredericksburg.

There he was surprised to find such a well-established community. All around town heavy German accents disturbed his memory, but he could not recall why. He rode past the Nimitz Hotel, went into Kammlah's store, and introduced himself to the short, round-faced storekeeper, who gave his name as Otto.

"What is that odd building?" Jeff asked, pointing to an octagonal structure in the middle of Main Street. "I've never seen anything like it."

"It is the Vereins Kirche." Otto chuckled. "We call is Die Kaffe-Muehle because with its eight sides it looks like a coffee mill."

"What is it used for?" Jeff asked.

"It was one of the first buildings in town and serves as a church, school, community hall, and fortress. When our people came here, they wanted a place to continue their religious faiths and to give their children an education."

"Who were the first settlers?"

"They came to take up land bought and given to them by a society of princes in Germany. Each settler received a 100 by 200-foot town lot and a ten-acre out lot to be used as a farm. They were allowed only one trunk to a family. The trunks were about 4 feet by 2 feet by 30 inches high and held all the family could bring in the way of household goods and clothing."

"That's amazing!" Jeff exclaimed. "American pioneers came west with a wagonload of family belongings and some livestock."

In another transient wisp of memory, Jeff saw a wagon piled high with household goods and the shadowy figure of a woman on horseback driving hogs before her.

Otto continued his history of Fredericksburg. "People headed to California during the 1849 Gold Rush stopped here because it was the last place they could buy supplies. Of course, this was good for the local merchants."

Jeff edged away while Otto was still prating and tipped his hat. "Good talking to you, Otto."

After lingering in Fredericksburg , Jeff moved on and began to ask for farm work and a place to stay; but none of the settlers on their out lots needed help. Further down the road he came to a cabin that looked more like that of the typical frontier settler than the German homes. Out front a man in overalls with chewing tobacco spilling down his gray beard sat with scuffed boots propped up on the porch rail.

"Howdy stranger," the man greeted Jeff. He pointed to a bench beside his own straight-back chair. "Light and set."

Jeff accepted the invitation, saying "I'm Jeff Barber from the Lazy Hawk."

"Never heard of it."

"I'm on my way back and looking for somebody to swap me a place to sleep and eat for work."

"I'm known as Tumbleweed Jones," the old man drawled. "People just call me Jones. Got no work, son, but plenty of grub and room to sleep. I'd be glad of your company for a spell."

"Thanks, Jones. How come you're on this land in the midst of all these Germans?"

"When money from that Society in Germany ran out, most of 'em pitched in and worked hard to make it here, but some wuz so discouraged they sold their grants for a few dollars. That's how I got this place."

After a supper of tinned beans, fried bacon, and cornbread, Jones washed the tin plates and cups and the iron skillet and motioned Jeff to follow him outside. It was early and unseasonably warm for Easter weekend and rapidly growing dark.

"Something out there you ought to see." Jones pointed toward the hills.

As Jeff watched, the hills sprang to life with dozens of fires. "What in all that's holy is that?" he asked.

"Easter fires." Jones chuckled. "Local custom that goes back to the days of the treaty with the Comanches. While they were meeting with the settlers from Fredericksburg, the Indians lit signal fires in the hills to send messages to each other."

"But why fires today?"

"A local custom. Story goes that a mother in town made up this story to calm her small youngun, who was afraid. Told the child the fires was lit by the Easter bunny to dye eggs. Now every year we light the Easter fires in the hills."

"If that don't beat all. The children must love it."

"They look forward to the fires every Easter and think about that old bunny out there dyeing them eggs, but I'm worried this year. Been such a long dry spell, the whole countryside could go up in flames if the wind gets up."

"How would you stop it? Can't hardly carry enough water to put out a fire in a house or barn much less in open country."

"First you plow a fire brake and pray for rain or a change of wind."

"What if that don't work?"

"Well, I seen folks slaughter cattle, skin 'em, and drag the carcasses across the edge of the fire. Then they come along with brooms and sacks and beat out the sparks. Never saw one that big, but I heard tell once of a 20-cow fire."

"I pray I never see nothing like that." Jeff shuddered and turned to go inside. Jones followed.

Tuesday after Easter Jones and Jeff sat at the kitchen table at two in the afternoon wolfing down beans and cornbread dipped in sorghum molasses and drinking great gulps of buttermilk. They had been up since before sunrise tilling the cultivated portion of Jones' land for spring planting, and their mid-day break was overdue.

The day was unseasonably warm, and the air pressed against their sweat-streaked faces heavy with moisture. The sun hid behind pewter clouds, and the overcast was tinged with yellow. Jeff was reminded of something, but the wisp of memory refused to take shape.

"Feel's like a storm brewing," he remarked.

"Yep," Jones agreed. "Good thing you put Chance in the barn. I better get old Bess and Rowdy to shelter."

"Want some help?"

"Nah. You clean up these here dishes. I kin handle that old cow and one stubborn mule."

"Better hurry," Jeff urged as he peered through the window at black clouds swirling overhead.

Jones penned Bess in the barn. Then as he began to tug at Rowdy's halter, the clouds exploded, spilling torrents of rain into the barnyard. The mule backed his ears and refused to budge. Jeff, watching from the cabin, could imagine the colorful epithets Jones was peppering on the ornery creature.

By the time Rowdy finally started toward the barn, hail mingled with the rain. The first stones were small, but within seconds chunks of ice the size of baseballs were battering the barnyard. Felled by blows to the head, Rowdy collapsed in his tracks. Jones dived for shelter beneath the water trough and lay where he fell with his left leg twisted and exposed to the pounding hail.

As soon as the hailstorm had passed over, Jeff rushed out to help the old man. He was unconscious but breathing, and his ankle turned out at a grotesque angle that spelled a broken leg. Carefully Jeff slid the inert form clear of the trough and immobilized Jones' leg with a bandanna wrapped around two flat pieces of kindling from the woodpile.

The old man outweighed Jeff by at least 40 pounds. Unconscious and a dead weight, he was a greater burden than Jeff could carry all the way to the cabin. He dared not drag him across the rough terrain and risk further injury to the leg. An idea took shape in Jeff's mind as a shadowy memory prodded him with a glimpse of red-skinned figures pulling a travois behind a horse.

Quickly Jeff lashed together a framework and covered it with a saddle blanket. Next he saddled Chance, led him from the barn, and secured the makeshift litter. Then he eased Jones aboard and slowly led Chance to the cabin.

He managed to lift the old man into the cabin, where he stripped him of his wet clothing and covered him with blankets. Then Jeff changed into a dry shirt and pants and brewed a strong pot of chamomile tea. The aroma served to revive Jones, and he began to moan and stir about. Jeff gave him a healthy portion of hot tea laced with whisky.

"Lie still, Jones. Your leg's broke."

"Sorry dern mule!" Jones cursed. "I'll have his hide."

"No use threatening Rowdy. Poor critter's dead."

"Killed by them giant hailstones," Jones mused. "Could have been me, I reckon."

"Well, it wasn't. Now we have to get some help with your leg."

"I've had some experience with broken bones. Just give me lots of whisky, lad, for the pain and have a go at setting this leg."

Coached by Jones, Jeff aligned the bones, splinted the leg in place, and bound it securely. The old man screamed only once but lay still during the whole procedure. Sweat poured down his face, and he spent a restless night but managed to eat some breakfast the following morning.

After Jeff cleaned up the dishes, he told Jones, "You need a doctor to look at this leg. Is there anyone we can send into Fredericksburg?"

"Young Bert Hasseldorf at the next farm could go. They got so many kids they'd never miss him. Be sure to tell them to help themselves to my peaches when they get ripe. The missus could use extra food, and they're too proud to ask."

"Will you be all right until I get back?"

"Yep. I'm tough as a old boot," Jones assured Jeff.

Bert was glad to fetch the doctor and Miz Hasseldorf's face brightened at the invitation to pick peaches. Now all they could do was wait. It was not until the next day that Herr Doctor Steiner arrived in his buggy and examined Jones.

"Young man, you did a goot job with der leg," he assured Jeff. "And you, Herr Jones, must keep off it till it heals."

"How long will that be?" Jones asked the doctor.

"I vill tell you when. Meantime, I come by vonce a week and check on you."

"Danka. Thanks, Herr Doctor."

Days stretched into weeks before Jones was able to get around with a crude crutch that Jeff fashioned for him. Meanwhile Jeff took care of everything around the place. At the end of the day he would sit with Jones and listen to stories of the old man's life and share the few details he could remember of his own.

One evening Jones prompted Jeff for more information. "You never mention anything about your life before Quail Run. How come?"

"Because I can't remember," Jeff confessed.

Then he poured out the story of how he lost his memory and took on the name Jeff Barber.

"I don't know who I am, how old I am, if I'm married or have a family. For all I know, I could be wanted by the law. It's awful!"

"Don't fret, son. I don't believe you done nothing bad. Some day you'll get yer mem'ry back and everthing will be clear."

"I've about lost hope."

With the exception of the brief hailstorm that had injured Jones, there had been no rainfall since the first of the year. Pastures were parched, and streams and stock tanks were drying up. There was no grass and few weeds. Ribs stood out on undernourished cattle, and armadillo claws could not pierce the hard earth.

Jeff grew increasingly restless, cooped up in the cabin so much to tend to Jones; but he was determined to see the old man through to recovery. Meals and dishes and washing were an unwelcome change from riding the range at the Lazy Hawk or working beside Sophie in her office. She was often in his thoughts, and he yearned to see her even if he had to keep his distance. He longed for the sound of her voice and a glimpse of her face. He missed Cal, too.

Finally Jones was able to limp around without his crutch, and Dr. Steiner pronounced him healed. Bert Hasseldorf was recruited to help with the heavier chores until Jones regained his strength, and Jeff was free to be on his way to the Lazy Hawk.

"Take a extra canteen from the barn and top off your water every place you can," Jones cautioned Jeff. "Drought has dried up most everything in the whole western part of the state. You'll be hard pressed to find water and grazing for Chance."

"This is the worst dry spell I can imagine, but we'll get by," Jeff assured him.

"Worst in twenty years," Jones told him. "You probably ain't been around that long."

The reminder that he did not know his age weighed heavily on Jeff as he rode through parched pasture land. If only I could remember, he kept thinking.

The sun was a beast on Jeff's back, and sweat soaked his shirt. Tumbleweeds tossed fitfully across brown landscape, and no oasis appeared on the horizon. The water in one canteen was gone, and in the other dangerously low. Chance had slaked his thirst a few miles back in a stagnant, nearly dry pond; but Jeff dared not drink from the shallow, slime-encrusted water for fear it would make him sick.

He pressed on until late afternoon with heat haze shimmering just ahead on the trail, which he could hardly distinguish from the barren land on either side. Once or twice he thought he sighted water; but when he approached, it was only a mirage. Bones of dead cattle bleaching in the sun told the story of drought and starvation. Jeff was glad he had a goodly supply of jerky, for no game presented itself.

He watched the orange-hued sun drop like a ball below the distant horizon. Then something ahead on his right caught his attention in the twilight. As he drew nearer, it proved to be a cabin flanked by a barn and a windmill giving an occasional lazy turn in the hot evening breeze.

Anticipation gave way to alarm when he saw that the cabin door flopped back and forth from time to time and the windows were shuttered. There was no livestock in the barn, and arrows lay scattered in the yard. When he reached the cabin door, he gagged at the smell of rotting flesh from within. He forced himself to step inside and almost stumbled over the corpses of a man and a woman, throats slit and scalps peeled away.

He rushed outside and retched, then found a shovel in the barn and dug two graves. When they were deep enough, he tied his bandanna over his nose and mouth, rolled the bodies in two quilts from the bed, and dragged them outside. Next he opened the shutters, propped open the door, and lighted two candles on the kitchen table to absorb the odor. Perhaps by morning, he could explore the kitchen without gagging.

With the bandanna still covering his nose and mouth, Jeff forced himself to maneuver the rotting corpses to their graves and roll them in. After covering them with dirt, he paused and prayed. "Receive, oh Lord, these Thy servants whose names are not known to me. If there were children in the family captured by savages, be merciful unto them. Amen."

The windmill was still pumping water. Jeff took a long drink from the dipper hanging there, filled both canteens, and poured water in the trough for Chance. After a supper of jerky he snuggled down in his bedroll and was soon asleep.

The next morning he made a hurried trip into the kitchen and brought outside coffee, moldy bacon, salt and meal, along with a frying pan and coffee pot. Never had a campfire breakfast of bacon and fried hoecake tasted so good. Chance had his fill of hay from the barn, and after that Jeff hit the trail again bound for the Lazy Hawk.

Chapter 9
FIRE AND SLEET

When Jeff finally reached the pastures of the Lazy Hawk, he found them as desolate as the countryside he had been traversing. Where once fat cattle roamed deep in green forage, dead grass spiked with dried weeds formed dangerous tinder. Here and there a few forlorn longhorns huddled in the shade of scattered trees with ribs showing against their hide and little prospect of nourishment from the scattered prickly pear plants.

He spurred Chance forward, dreading what he would find at ranch headquarters. There in the corral several dozen lean steers milled dejectedly around an empty feed trough. The once lush garden near the house drooped and withered in the sun. The windmill circled lazily and creaked an apology that it could not pump enough water to save the vegetables from the relentless drought that had West Texas in its grip.

Jeff pulled Chance to a halt at the house, leaped from the saddle, and looped the reins around the porch rail. He took the steps two at a time, calling "Sophie! Cal!"

The door flew open, and Cal flung himself on Jeff and wrapped around his legs. At the same time Sophie sprang into his arms sobbing. "Where in Heaven's name have you been? We thought you weren't coming back."

Jeff held her close for a moment, then summoned the strength to release her from the embrace.

"It's a long story, and it can wait. First tell me what's happened here. From what I saw riding in, things look mighty bad."

Sophie flushed and composed herself. "Come in and we'll talk." She turned to Cal. "Take care of Jeff's horse."

Jeff followed Sophie inside, where they sat down side by side in the office as they were wont to do. A longing look passed between them, but they were careful not to touch. Jeff wished he could just resign himself to leaving his past blank and marry Sophie, but it would not be fair when he had no idea who he was nor how old he was nor whether he had a family.

Without words Sophie handed him the books for the past months of ranch operation. The longer Jeff studied the figures, the deeper he frowned.

"Curse this drought! You're near ruined."

She nodded. "Most of the men have moved on to find other jobs. I couldn't pay them, and there was nothing for them to do anyway. I sold most of the stock at rock-bottom prices to keep them from starving."

"Are you feeding those steers in the corral?" Jeff asked.

"As long as the hay stored in the barn lasts." A single tear trickled down Sophie's cheek. "We rotate the stock in the corral with the stock left on the range. We'll have to drive them all to market soon while they can still walk."

"How many men stayed on?"

"Just Boggs and Shorty."

"What about Maria, the old woman who used to clean and do the washing?"

"She took her daughter home to Mexico. I manage to do her work with some help from Cal. He pitched right in when he realized how serious our situation is."

"I know how bad you want to keep the Lazy Hawk going for him."

"If his father were only here, he'd know what to do."

"Sophie, you're doing the best anybody could. Nobody can fight this long drought. It's about ruined everybody from here to Fredericksburg."

"I don't know how things can get any worse," Sophie muttered.

They were soon to find out.

The next few days were overcast, and humidity pressed against their bodies like steam from a kettle. The occasional roll of distant thunder tantalized them, but still no rain came. On the third day Jeff and Sophie and Cal stood on the veranda scanning the horizon for hope of a shower. Pitchforks of lightning stabbed closer and closer to the dry ground, etching fear on Sophie's face.

Suddenly Cal jumped up and down and pointed to a distant pasture. "Look, Mama! Fire!"

As far as they could see, the landscape surrounding the flash of fire was a flat, dusty brown, punctuated at intervals with tall, withered weeds. It made a perfect canvas for wildfire to paint its tongues of orange and yellow.

Jeff rushed toward the barn, shouting, "We've got to plow a fire brake!"

Ahead of him Shorty was already hitching a pair of mules to the plow. They seemed to sense the urgency of the moment and responded by allowing the little man to drive them without their usual balking. Shorty drove the team a hundred yards west of the ranch buildings and turned up a twisted ribbon of earth to cover the dry grass and weeds. Then he retraced his path in the opposite direction and kept plowing back and forth until a wide arc of dirt separated the dry grass on either side.

When the brake seemed wide enough, Shorty and Jeff joined Boggs in the barnyard and watched the progress of the fire. Flames were zigzagging across dry grass and weeds and licking greedily at the trees dotting the pasture of the Lazy Hawk. A giant oak exploded from the boil of its sap, and clouds of birds darkened the air flying eastward toward safety. Jackrabbits, possums, and raccoons raced from the underbrush ahead of the fire. Cattle in the pasture stampeded before the flames, and the odor of singed hides was strong on the stiff wind blowing toward the barn.

On the porch of the ranch house Sophie and Cal coughed and rubbed their eyes. It was plain that the wind whipping the flames in their direction would soon boost burning cinders across the fire brake.

Jeff shared with Boggs and Shorty the story of the 20-cow fire that Tumbleweed Jones had described, and they agreed that it was time to try extreme measures.

"Saddle up," Boggs directed. "Bring ropes and brooms and feed sacks.

"There's dying animals aplenty lying at the edge of the fire," Shorty observed.

As the three men rode toward the fire brake, cinders were already blowing across its width and igniting patches of grass inside the brake. Several steers had made it to the brake before collapsing. They were moving their legs feebly, and a single shot to the head quickly ended their misery.

Jeff and Shorty and Boggs skinned three of the dead animals and tied one behind each of their horses. Then they dragged the heavy mess across the flames springing to life wherever cinders had fallen inside the fire brake. As soon as the flames died down, the riders dismounted and began to beat out the remaining sparks with brooms and feed sacks.

Their task appeared to be hopeless. No sooner was one fire extinguished than another sprang up. The ranch buildings seemed doomed.

Jeff rode back to the house and yelled to Sophie, "If the fire reaches the barn, be ready to abandon the house. Saddle your horse and Cal's pony now and tie them to the porch rail."

She headed to the stable and shouted back over her shoulder. "No telling how far east we'll have to ride to outrun the fire."

The boy started to follow his mother, but Jeff turned his horse to block the way. "Cal, you wait right here, and don't move till your mama gets back. You hear me!"

"Aw, all right, Jeff."

As far as he could see, storm clouds were gathering overhead, bringing Jeff a glimmer of hope. A fork of lightning speared one of the remaining trees in the far pasture, and thunder pealed like the chuck wagon dinner bell on a cookout. Just as a spark flared on the roof of the barn, the clouds spilled their load of rain, loosing torrents across the Lazy Hawk. In short order the blazing pastures and smoldering grass inside the fire brake were reduced to a soggy mass running with water,

"Yippee!" Cal yelled as he bounded from the porch. "Sky juice!"

"Praise be to God!" Sophie shouted. "We're saved."

"Miz Sophie, you deserve a bit of luck!" Shorty croaked, wiping black smudges from his face with his red bandanna.

"A few minutes longer, and all the ranch buildings would have gone up in smoke," Boggs muttered.

The owner of the Lazy Hawk shook each man's hand. "Thank you from the bottom of my heart for what you did. You bought us enough time until the rains came."

"We wuz glad to help." Shorty spoke for all of them.

"Let's go in and wash up, and I'll rustle us up some grub," Sophie offered.

"Hurry, mama," Cal urged. "I'm starving."

"First let's see what we can salvage in the way of meat and hides from the dead cattle," Jeff suggested. "Plenty of time to eat later."

Several hours later darkness settled over the landscape, and still it rained. The rain continued throughout the night, soaking the parched Lazy Hawk and raising the spirits of those who had saved it.

During the weeks that followed Jeff drove to market most of Sophie's remaining cattle after helping Boggs and Shorty cull those kept to start a new herd. When this was done, there was nothing more for him to do. Sophie no longer needed an assistant to keep the pitifully few ranch records, and the two older men could easily handle the remnant of the livestock.

One day he said to Sophie, "I'll be heading out to Fort Worth tomorrow. Maybe there's work in Tarrant County."

The next morning when he was ready to go, she squeezed his arm. "I'll miss you terribly, but I know I can't keep you here."

"When I find out who I really am, maybe I'll come back." Jeff resisted the urge to kiss her good-bye.

"The Mexicans have a saying--Que será será." Sophie said. "Vaya con dios."

Although the day was temperate, Jeff carried a warm jacket and a slicker across his saddle. "Remember," Sophie reminded him, "November in West Texas can be unpredictable. Travel with an eye on the weather."

Sunshine-filled days followed one after another, and Jeff reached Buffalo Gap on the Callahan Divide in Taylor County. He followed the well-defined trail etched by millions of buffalo feet long before cowpokes drove longhorns along the Dodge Trail from Texas to Kansas.

Beyond the gap he found himself skirting flat-topped mesas that stood above the plains like rough-hewn tables. He supposed that in the spring the landscape would be softened by muted desert colors and low vegetation, but now it was bleak and forbidding. With no warning, the wind shifted and the temperature dropped rapidly. A blue norther threatened to pry him from the saddle, and he looked about in vain for some sheltering cabin or sign of human habitation.

Sheets of sleet followed on the heels of the bitter wind, stinging his face and reducing visibility to zero. Chance began to slip on the icy ground, and Jeff edged him closer to the juncture of two adjoining mesas he had noted before the storm hit. He thought there might be an opening where they nearly overlapped and pinned his hopes on locating an overhang that would shelter him.

Sleet was accumulating in piles along the sides of the mesa when he reached a shadowy spot that stood out from the white pellets edging it. He urged Chance forward and discovered a small cave just large enough to accommodate a man and a horse. It's mouth was partially obscured by underbrush, which he quickly dragged inside and heaped near the entrance to start a fire.

Jeff rubbed Chance down and reclined close to the fire, warming his hands and his feet. He was beginning to feel relaxed and drowsy when he was startled upright by an unmistakable rattle that drove splinters of fear down his spine. Not two feet away a diamond-back rattlesnake, disturbed from its hibernation and drawn by warmth, slithered along the edge of the rocks and moved toward the fire.

Jeff jumped up and reached for his gun, but the snake was quicker. He felt a sharp pain as it struck just above the top of his boot and knew he would die if the venom spread. Pausing just long enough to blow off the rattler's head with a single shot, he grabbed a stick and his bandanna and twisted it into a tourniquet above the wound.

Jeff grasped the tourniquet firmly in his left hand and sterilized his Bowie knife in the fire with his right. When it cooled, he made two deep cuts directly across the wound and pressed firmly in all directions around the bite until blood flowed freely onto the ground. The pain combined with the sight of so much of his own blood caused him to retch violently, but he continued his efforts to rid his bloodstream of venom.

At intervals Jeff loosened the tourniquet and tightened it again. Throughout the long night he shivered and shook but thought if he could live through the next two days he would survive. The next morning he risked standing to drag in more brush for the fire, and by evening he felt the worst had passed. He had skinned the snake and from time to time cut off chunks and roasted them over the fire. Rattlesnake steak was a welcome change from cold jerky.

As soon as he felt up to the effort, he tied a rope to Chance and slapped him on the rump, encouraging him to go outside the cave and graze where the ice had begun to thaw in patches. By the third day, Jeff was feeling stronger, and the sun had melted much of the ice outside.

He mounted Chance and again set out toward Fort Worth, avoiding the treacherous patches of ice remaining in shaded areas. Once again the sun sat warm on his shoulders, and it was hard to believe how cold it had been just a short time before. Jeff was reminded of a saying the old timers had: "If you don't like the weather in Texas, just wait a few minutes."

Chapter 10
A CLOSE CALL

On the third day Jeff had just passed through a grove of live oaks when he saw a buggy overturned up ahead and a woman seated beside it alternately cursing and weeping.

"What happened, ma'am?"

"That bastard mare spooked and ran away with me. Turned me plumb over." She gave the buggy a kick. "I got old Queen here unhitched but can't seem to set this thing upright on its wheels."

Jeff saw that the woman was sturdily built and amply proportioned but no longer young. A pair of small, round, wire-rimmed glasses perched on her nose; and a faded print sunbonnet sat askew atop iron gray hair.

"I'll be glad to help you, ma'am." Jeff dismounted and approached the buggy.

"Thank you. I kin sure use some help." The woman wiped her forehead with her sleeve and offered her hand. "I'm Mattie Archer from near Comanche. Everbody calls me Miss Mattie, so I reckon you can."

"Glad to meet you, Miss Mattie. I'm Jeff Barber, and I'm headed for Fort Worth." He shook her hand, then placed a shoulder beneath the edge of the buggy and easily righted it.

"Thank you kindly, Jeff. Are you in a hurry to get to Fort Worth?"

"Not really. I'm just looking for a place to earn my keep." Jeff smiled at the broad, friendly face beneath the worn bonnet.

"I could sure use somebody like you around my place. Since my old man died and the children growed up and left, the chores just keep piling up. Can't pay you nothing, but I'll feed you good and give you a place to sleep."

Jeff grinned. "That's the best offer I've had all day. Lead the way."

When they reached the settlement of Comanche, Miss Mattie told Jeff it had once been a campground for Comanche Indians. She pointed with a callused finger to a "picket house" of logs cut and split on the ground and set vertically in a ditch. "That there's the courthouse. This has been the county seat since '58."

"It don't look like much," Jeff observed.

"This ain't Austin," Miss Mattie reminded him. "It's still Indian country."

A few miles beyond the town they arrived at Miss Mattie's home. Jeff saw in a wink how far the place had run down. The front door sagged on one hinge, and the rotted porch floor had a hole big enough to drop a skunk through. Shutters banged against windows without latches, and the whole house was badly in need of a coat of whitewash.

Jeff went to work at daybreak the next morning with hammer and nails, tightening hinges and replacing boards. He cleaned the outhouse and buried the accumulated feces in a field away from the house. By the time he finished reinforcing the rails around the hog pen, it was early afternoon and he was ripe with sweat.

Miss Mattie called to him from the yard, where she was spreading wet clothes. "Time to quit. Rome warn't built in a day, as they say. By the time you get scrubbed up under the pump there, I'll have the vittles ready."

When Jeff sat down at the kitchen table across from Miss Mattie, he faced the best meal he had eaten in a very long time, fried chicken, cornbread, gravy, and sweet potatoes. "Miss Mattie, you sure cook good. I feel like I died and went to heaven."

"Go on with you, Jeff. Ain't been nobody but me here in a long time, and I'm kinda out of practice."

"With no help around the place how do you manage to farm?"

"Couple of neighbors come over from town to work the land on a share basis. Don't guess you'd stay on and do that?"

"I'll think on it, Miss Mattie," Jeff promised.

Days stretched into weeks, and still Jeff stayed on, whitewashing, nailing loose boards, and sprucing up the place. He took to going into town with Miss Mattie to the Campbellite church until one Sunday in mid-December the sunshine and unseasonable warmth of the day called him to work outdoors. While Miss Mattie got ready for church, he nailed down wire mesh that had come loose from the wooden frames around the chicken coops, then rode Chance down beyond the creek to check on old Bossy and her new calf.

At mid-day Jeff started back to the farmhouse looking forward to one of Miss Mattie's special Sunday dinners. When he penned Chance in the barnyard, he noticed that the buggy was still where he had left it for her and Old Queen was nowhere to be seen. A premonition of something amiss caused him to hasten his steps to the house, and a silent alarm sounded in his head when he found the back screen door torn and flopping back and forth.

When Jeff strode into the kitchen, he nearly stumbled over Miss Mattie. She lay prone on the plank floor, left arm flung out, the right bent beneath her ample breast. Her head was cocked slightly to one side, and blood welled from a small cut on her temple. Even before he felt for her pulse, Jeff knew she was dead. A narrow band of white skin around the suntanned third finger of her left hand caught his attention, and he realized he had never before seen her not wearing her wedding ring.

Jeff looked around the room, noting a tiny smear of blood on the sharp corner of the kitchen table. Near the stove a spill of bacon fat streaked the floor, and the iron skillet lay upside down beside it. He picked it up just as he heard Doc Thompson's voice at the front door.

"Miss Mattie, are you all right?"

Then Deacon Hollister's bass added, "We missed you at church and come out to see about you."

"Come on in," Jeff called to the men. "She's in the kitchen."

The presence of the corpse in the kitchen had unsettled him even more than the gory bodies of the nameless settlers he had buried. This was someone he knew, someone of whom he had grown fond. He was standing motionless with the skillet in his hand staring at Miss Mattie on the floor when the men from church walked in, hats in their hands.

"My God! What have you done?" Doc's voice was rough with anger.

"I found her like this," Jeff explained. For the first time he noticed the single strand of red hair clinging to the edge of the skillet where grease had trickled down the side. "She's dead."

"I can see that," Doc thundered. "Looks like her neck's broke."

"How long ago" Hollister asked.

""'Don't rightly know," Doc admitted. "It'd take some fancy city doctor with a lab to determine exact time of death."

Jeff laid down the skillet and started to the bedroom to get a blanket to cover Miss Mattie's body, but Doc stepped in front of him."Hold on, Barber. You're coming with us."

"What for?" Fear clutched at Jeff's belly as he realized how guilty he must look.

"To see the county sheriff," Doc told him.

"Hollister grabbed Jeff by the arm and glared. "This looks pretty cut and dried. You're the only one here, and the skillet you hit her with was still in your hand when we come in."

"Now why would I want to hit her?" Jeff protested. "She's been a good friend to me."

"Maybe for the little bit of cash she always keeps around," Doc suggested.

"I haven't touched it. She keeps it in the sugar bowl on the top shelf," Jeff volunteered.

"Let's have a look." Doc set the bowl painted with pink roses on the kitchen table and removed the lid.

"Empty!" Hollister exclaimed.

"That settles it," Doc told Jeff as he shoved him through the door.

"Saddle your horse, and don't try no funny stuff."

Jeff looked from the corpse to Doc and avowed, "I swear I didn't kill her."

A few minutes later the three men started to Comanche, Jeff riding between the other two. Halfway there they noticed someone on horseback lurking in the shadows of a grove of pecan trees, and Jeff spurred Chance ahead of the others in that direction.

"Look! He's riding Old Queen!" Jeff shouted, adding under his breath, "And he has red hair."

The rider broke from the trees and galloped down the path, but old Queen was no match for Chance. Jeff soon overtook the other rider and pulled him to the ground.

"Who the hell are you?" Jeff demanded.

"Esker Archer," the man panted as he lay glowering at Jeff towering above him.

Doc, who had followed swift on Jeff's heels, pulled up his horse and looked down at the pockmarked face beneath a thatch of straggly, carrot-colored hair.

"Esker Archer! I never thought you'd show your face around here again."

Deacon Hollister caught up with the others in time to add, "Not after you stole from your uncle while working his farm and he made you git!"

"Who is this Esker Archer?" Jeff asked.

"Black sheep of the Archer family. A nephew of Miss Mattie's husband," Doc explained.

Doc looked from Jeff to Archer. "He would know, same as you, where Miss Mattie kept her cash."

Jeff placed one booted foot on Esker's chest and ordered, "Empty your pockets."

The redhead hesitated, then turned his pockets inside out. A shower of coins scattered in the dirt. Reaching down among them, Jeff picked up a shiny gold circle with a hole in the center.

"Miss Mattie's wedding ring!"

"I didn't mean to kill her, "Esker Archer whined. "Just needed a little money for Christmas. I knew she kept some in the sugar bowl and figured she'd be at church. I just got there too soon before she left."

Jeff fought back a tear. "You had no need to kill her."

"It wuz a accident. She caught me red-handed in the kitchen and whopped me on the head with the skillet. I shoved her, and she hit her head on the table. When I saw she was done for, I took her mare and high-tailed it."

Hollister stepped forward and tied Esker's hands behind his back. "Start marching, and get ready to tell your story to the sheriff."

Then Hollister turned to Jeff. "You lead Old Queen home, and we'll take this sorry piece of humanity into Comanche to stand trial."

Doc offered Jeff his hand. "Sorry we accused you. You got to admit circumstances looked bad for you."

Sweat beaded on Jeff's forehead. "If I hadn't of happened to spot that Esker was on Old Queen, I might have hung for murder!"

A few days after Mattie Archer's funeral Jeff shook the dirt of Comanche from his boots and resumed his trek toward Fort Worth.

Chapter 11
TUTORING IN FORT WORTH

When Jeff rode into Fort Worth on a Saturday afternoon, he was shocked to find the town dying. The only signs of life were dance halls, saloons, and brothels. Most of the Tarrant County offices were abandoned. No officers patrolled the streets, and the jail was empty. O'Hara's Mercantile on a side street bore a forlorn "Open" sign, which encouraged Jeff to go inside. Shelves were mostly bare, but a crudely-lettered sign on the counter announced prices for certain commodities. Flour - $15/100 lbs. Corn - $2/bu. Pork - $20/100 lbs. Cloth - $4-$5/yd.

Jeff was turning to leave when a voice spoke from a dark corner of the store. "What can I do for you?"

"Where is everybody? Last I heard Fort Worth was a thriving county seat with maybe 6,000 people."

"Used to be. Most of 'em gone now." The proprietor stepped around the counter and offered his hand. "I'm Sean O'Hara."

Jeff shook O'Hara's callused hand. "I'm Jeff Barber, here looking for work. What happened to all the people?"

"War, Indians, and the depression. Soldiers keep commandeering beef for the army. They cull herds of all beeves over four year old. If a rancher takes a shot at the soldiers on his land, he's hung for treason."

"Many hangings?" Jeff asked.

"Too many. Confederates hang anybody who's against slavery. Call them Union sympathizers even if they are for the South."

"How many are left in town?" Jeff asked.

"About 250," O'Hara replied. "Private schools closed for lack of tutors, and families moved back east."

"Most folks want their younguns to get some education," Jeff observed.

O'Hara squared his shoulders. "A few hardy souls are hanging on in spite of everything. I try to keep 'em provisioned."

"I guess getting work on a ranch or in a store is out of the question with things so depressed." Jeff looked around at the empty shelves.

"I'm sorry, son." O'Hara clasped Jeff's shoulder in a gesture of comfort.

"I'm adaptable." Jeff grinned. "Do you suppose I could do some tutoring for bed and food. I read tolerably well and am good with sums."

"You're the answer to a prayer! Let me be the first to take you in. I got a brood of five, ages 6 to 15. Neighbors have another dozen. Between us, we can keep you fed and give you a place to sleep. No salary, I'm afraid."

"Bed and board'll do just fine." Jeff exhaled rapidly, relieved to find a way to stay on in Fort Worth.

"I'm ready to close up. Let's go home for supper and find you a place to sleep."

Fifteen minutes later, Jeff mounted Chance and followed O'Hara's sorrel mare through town. The tinny strains of a saloon piano and high-pitched laughter drew his attention down a side street, where painted girls leaned out second-story windows. He had never seen a fancy lady before, and he stared long and hard at the bevy of soiled doves.

O'Hara saw where Jeff was looking and warned, "That's Hell's Half Acre. Decent folk don't linger there."

Jeff flushed and changed the subject. "Anything exciting happen around here now that the town's dying?"

"Not since December of sixty when Capt. Ross and some Texas

Rangers and members of the U. S. Second Cavalry whipped the Comanches and recaptured Cynthia Ann Parker."

"Who's she?" Jeff asked.

"A little girl stole by the Indians back in 1836."

A splinter of memory caught in Jeff's mind, and for an instant he saw two naked white children running before him to escape being roped. As quickly as it came, the picture faded into limbo, and O'Hara was telling him more about Cynthia Ann Parker.

"She growed up as a Indian, was Chief Quanah Parker's squaw, and considered herself one of them. After the soldiers took her, the poor thing went to her uncle, Col. Isaac Parker, in Birdville near here. He had to lock her up at night to keep her from returning to the Indians."

"Did you ever see her?" Jeff asked.

"Yep. Her and her child, Prairie Flower, was on display once here in Fort Worth. She was dressed in calico and bound with a rope. When I saw her, she was standing on a wooden box, looking heartbroken. You'd have thought she was a Indian 'cept for her blonde hair. It was straight cut and shoulder length."

"That's pathetic! What became of her?"

"They sent her to her brother, Silas Parker, Jr., in Anderson County over in East Texas. Last I heard she was still trying to escape."

On the outskirts of town O'Hara dismounted at a whitewashed two-story house and motioned to Jeff to follow him inside.

"Missus O'Hara, set another plate for supper. This here's Jeff Barber. He'll be staying with us and tutoring the children," the host explained.

"Saints preserve us! You're the answer to a prayer." Mrs. O'Hara's smile lighting up her round, rosy face was the most welcome sight Jeff had seen since he rode into Fort Worth. "I feared the little O'Haras would grow up in ignorance."

"Children, we have a guest," Mrs. O'Hara shouted up the stairwell. "Come on down and eat."

At her call, four little O'Haras rushed down the stairs, stumbling over each other in their haste to see who the guest might be.

Close behind them, but at a more leisurely pace, came a comely girl ready-made to turn young men's heads. She was no more than five feet, two inches tall with an exquisitely proportioned figure that even the drab linsey-woolsey dress she wore could not hide. Skin the color of fresh buttermilk and a halo of auburn curls set off a saucy pair of green eyes and a tip-tilted nose lightly dusted with freckles.

O'Hara introduced the siblings. "The younger ones are Paddy, Maureen, Gerald, and Timothy--in that order. The beauty of the bunch coming down last is me darling Molly."

Jeff's gaze riveted on Molly, and he stood speechless as though rooted to the floor.

She smiled and held out a dainty white hand. "How do you do, whoever you are." She hesitated, then mischievously dropped a curtsy.

"This is Jeff Barber," O'Hara announced. "He will be your new tutor."

"I--I'm pleased to meet you," Jeff stammered as he took Molly's hand. "I'm sure we'll get on well."

"I'm sure we will." Molly gave Jeff a bold wink.

"Enough of your shenanigans," Mrs. O'Hara scolded Molly. "Now all of you, come set down and bow your heads while your father says grace."

A chorus of amens followed the blessing of the food; and dishes of hot food passed quickly from hand to hand around the long, well-worn oak table that stretched the length of the kitchen. A platter of fried prairie chickens came first, followed by a bowl of lye hominy and cornbread with syrup made from watermelons.

"You're lucky, "Molly addressed their guest. "Somebody traded Pa these prairie chickens he shot on the banks of the Trinity. Sometimes we have liver pudding." She pulled her mouth down in disgust. "Ugh!"

"Prairie chickens and wild turkeys are plentiful, and bartering is about the only way to trade these days," O'Hara explained to Jeff. "Cash is in short supply, and there's not much to back up credit.

People often have to do without."

"I know something about that," Jeff said. "I drove a few head of cattle to Austin to trade for some supplies we needed on the Lazy Hawk."

Talking about that trip turned Jeff's thoughts back to the ranch, and he worried how Sophie and Cal were surviving the losses from the drought and the fire. He realized his concern was reflected in his face when Mrs. O'Hara spoke up.

"Mr. Barber, is something troubling you?"

"I was just thinking of friends who are having hard times," Jeff explained. "Southwest Texas has been hard hit by drought and prairie fires."

"I guess that's why you left," Mr. O'Hara remarked. "People are hard pressed here, too."

"The women are overworked," Mrs. O'Hara complained, "making bandages and knitting socks and mittens for our soldiers and sewing all the clothes for their families. You know how fast a passel of younguns can outgrow their britches."

Molly sighed. "I declare there's nothing fancy or pretty any more. Nothing but cotton shirts and pants, bed ticking suspenders, and linsey-woolsey dresses."

"The need for cloth was so great that some of the Masons tore joints from the first floor of the Lodge to make looms for the women," O'Hara told Jeff.

In the days that followed Jeff's tutoring proved challenging. After breakfast he would gather his small group of students together at one of their homes and work first on basics. Those with little previous schooling practiced phonics, handwriting, and addition and subtraction under the guidance of an older student already proficient in these areas. The intermediate learners worked on spelling, grammar, punctuation, multiplication tables, and division from books left behind by a former tutor, traveling light on his way back East.

Molly and another more advanced student tackled long division and read poetry, history and novels available from several families' bookshelves. Jeff moved among the groups, correcting and encouraging.

"Molly, you are an apt pupil," he told her one day. "What would you like to study next?"

"I'm hankering to study how to get you to notice me," Molly blurted out boldly, loud enough for all the others to hear.

Guffaws from the boys and titters from the girls swept around the class, and Jeff felt his face flush with embarrassment.

"Molly O'Hara, you're out of line. I'll be speaking with your father about your behavior."

"Go on and speak with him." Molly's eyes danced with devilment in a face as solemn as a deacon on Sunday. "I don't care just so long as you ask his permission to court me!"

Jeff closed the book in his hands with a bang. "Class dismissed!"

That evening after supper he waited until the younger children were excused before addressing his host.

"Mr. O'Hara, Molly disrupted class today. She seems to have fixed on me as a prospective suitor and made a spectacle of both of us."

"So the minx has set her cap for you, has she?" O'Hara grinned.

Jeff fidgeted with his fork. "Under the circumstances I think I should move on to another student's home."

"That can be arranged. I'll speak to the Thompsons."

Mrs. O'Hara rose and glared at her oldest daughter with an expression that could have soured milk.

"Molly Meagan O'Hara, apologize to Mr. Barber this instant. Then go to your room. I'll have no more of your wanton ways."

Molly stood up with a toss of auburn curls. "I do apologize because Mama says I must." She blew Jeff a kiss. "But I'm not sorry I want you to court me!"

With that she gathered up her skirts and ascended the staircase with a show of dignity that would have done credit to the preacher's wife on Sunday.

Secretly Jeff acknowledged to himself that if circumstances were different, he would be happy to court Molly O'Hara. Her fiery temperament and angelic face drew him like a nail to a magnet, and her lissome figure provoked similar feelings to those he had felt for Sophie. What would Molly think if she knew that all that kept him from crossing the line from tutor to suitor was not knowing who he was?

By the end of the week Jeff was settled with the Thompson family, sleeping on a cot in the room with their two oldest boys. He missed talking with Sean O'Hara and before long fell into the habit of stopping by the store in the afternoon to work beside the older man. He expected no pay and received none. He enjoyed the Irishman's company and the opportunity to be of some use when he would have otherwise been idle.

Soon after Jeff's move O'Hara asked him, "How do you like it at the Thompsons'?"

"It's a bit crowded, and meals aren't near so good as Mrs. O'Hara's." Jeff grinned and added, "But their oldest girl is just ten and not likely to have any notions about me."

O'Hara chuckled. "Don't be too sure."

"The Thompsons use sycamore balls soaked in oil instead of tallow candles," Jeff complained, "and drink substitute coffee made of parched barley and wheat."

"Not everybody is as fortunate as we are," O'Hara admitted. "We get a little coffee smuggled out of Mexico and can still afford tallow candles."

A few weeks later Molly lingered after lessons were over and spoke to Jeff in a respectful and demure pupil-to-teacher tone. "Mr. Barber, Pa was wondering if you might do him a favor."

"He knows I would. What's the favor?"

"He promised the younger kids they could go fishing in the Trinity this afternoon, and he'd like you to go along and watch out for them."

"Why can't you do it?"

"I wanted to, but Mama says I have to help with making preserves."

"Then I'll be glad to help."

"Thank you, Mr. Barber. I'll tell them to meet you in an hour in that big grove of cottonwoods near Miller's dock."

An hour later Jeff was waiting at the appointed place and hoping Mrs. O'Hara would send along some of her ham sandwiches for a snack. The children did not appear, and Jeff wondered how long he should wait.

"Surprise!" Molly stepped from the shadows behind a tree, dressed in a green muslin dress that must have come from her grandmother's trunk in the attic. She was wearing matching ribbons in her hair.

A warning bell sounded in Jeff's head. "What in thunder are you doing here? I come to meet the children."

"Came," Molly corrected.

"I came to meet the children." Jeff was chagrined that she had caught him using the incorrect verb form. The verbs prescribed by the grammar text often failed to spill over into common conversational usage. "The question is, what are you doing here?" he demanded.

Molly pursed her lips into a pout. "I just wanted to be alone with you, Jeff. That's why I invented the story about Pa needing a favor."

"You know well enough you shouldn't be here, Molly O'Hara. You may not be safe!"

"What could happen to me--unless maybe you was to kiss me?" So much for grammatical verb forms.

Jeff took her by the shoulders, bussed her soundly, then shook her. "I see I'll have to trust you with a secret. You must promise not to tell."

Molly's eyes widened, and she trailed a finger in an X along the swell of her left breast. "Cross my heart and hope to die."

"I'm not really Jeff Barber!"

Molly's eyebrows arched upward. "Then who are you?"

"I don't know. Maybe a killer or a bank robber, a married man with children, or someone evil who takes advantage of young girls alone in the woods." He approached her with an attempt to look menacing.

Molly backed a few steps away. "How come you don't know?"

"It seems I fell and struck my head. When I came to, I had lost all memory of my life to that point."

Molly retraced the steps she had taken away from Jeff and placed a small white hand on his arm. "You don't scare me, Jeff Barber, whoever you are. I don't believe you are bad, and I still feel the same about you."

She stepped closer, put her arms around his neck, and stood on tiptoe to reach his mouth with her lips. Resolved not to let the situation get out of hand, he gently unclasped her arms from his neck and stepped away.

"I'm not free to make any plans or any commitments to anybody until I know who I really am." He spoke in a voice husky with emotion.

"I understand," Molly assured him. "I'll just wait until you get your memory back."

Jeff was relieved that Molly's pursuit of him was on hold. Little did he suspect that she would betray his confidence and share his secret. The first inkling came when O'Hara cornered him one afternoon in the store.

"What's this nonsense about you maybe being a killer or a bank robber and not knowing who you really are?"

"How'd you find out?"

"I overheard Molly spinning yarns to her sister and swearing her to secrecy. You should a knowed she couldn't keep a secret."

"The part about losing my memory is true enough, though I doubt I'm wanted by the law. The rest of the story I sort of embroidered to scare Molly off."

"Well, it didn't work. According to what she told her sister, she thinks a lost memory is the most romantic thing in the world. She's just waiting for you to get your memory back so she can get the real you to court her."

"I give up!" Jeff threw up his hands. "I don't know what to do to discourage that girl of yours."

"She don't discourage easy," O'Hara admitted.

Conversation at the store often turned on the fact that many items wanted by customers were not available because no drummers were coming through town these days taking orders. One day while O'Hara was arranging stock, Jeff waited idly for a customer. None came until a stranger limped in and asked for some flour and beans. He was stooped and gray and wearing small wire-rimmed glasses, and his eyes darted around the empty shelves while Jeff was filling his order.

"I see you ain't got much in stock in the way of hard goods," he observed.

"True. We haven't found a source of supply lately," Jeff explained.

"You ought ter take a wagon and go east of Dallas to Canton on First Monday," the stranger suggested. "You wouldn't believe the stuff they got for sale. Saddles and bridles, dishes, pots and pans, tools, and wagons. None of it new, but plenty of good stuff."

"How far is it?"

"Two, maybe three days from here," the stranger estimated.

"Thanks," Jeff said as the stranger paid him and left with his purchases.

"Did you hear that?" Jeff called to the back of the store.

"Sure did," O'Hara answered. "Maybe I ought to take a wagon and check out them First Monday Trade Days. Will you go with me to Canton, Jeff?"

"Why not?" Jeff broke into a grin. "My students will be glad of a little holiday, and I could use a change."

"Better take your horse along in case I buy so much there's not enough room for you in the wagon coming back."

Chapter 12
RETURN OF THE PRODIGAL

When O'Hara and Jeff reached Canton, they found buyers trailing from vendor to vendor like ants toward sugar. There was every conceivable kind of merchandise for sale, and from all sides could be heard snatches of dickering and bargaining.

"I won't give you a cent more than two dollars."

"It's worth every penny I'm asking."

"How long you had it?"

"Don't make no difference. It's good as new."

"No it ain't. It's cracked."

"I'll trade you three hens for it."

O'Hara was delighted to find so many bargains to stock his store, and before his money was gone his wagon was nearly full. There were saddles and wash tubs, bowl and pitcher sets, hammers and saws and nails, bolts and nuts, lanterns, lengths of dress fabric, and ribbons for hats. Fancy parlor lamps hand painted with roses and pansies and ivy nestled in hand-pieced quilts to protect them from breakage on the trip back home.

Finally O'Hara turned to Jeff and said, "Let's go have a look at the dogs. I have a mind to take home a hound pup for the younguns."

"They'll be tickled pink."

They walked to the area where young litters of hunting dogs were displayed for sale, and Jeff waited while O'Hara made his selection.

His attention was drawn to a vendor who somehow looked familiar, though he did not remember ever seeing the man before. He was tall and burnt by years of sun, with a grizzled beard and commanding eyes. His voice was pitched to harangue a crowd, and Jeff was stirred by the familiar tones.

"This litter's from my favorite hound. My hounds are missionary dogs." He chuckled deep in his chest. "They travel with me to tree Campbellites so I can preach to them."

Something about the voice, the comment, the face bridged the gap in Jeff's broken memory. For the first time since his accident a scene from his past came clearly in focus and remained there. He was back at Camp Colorado listening to Robinson's interminable sermon that earned him the nickname Choctaw Bill.

While Jeff was remembering Robinson, for it was indeed he, the preacher turned his eyes in that direction and whooped, "Sam Houston Gossett! We thought you were dead. Last time I saw you, I thought you'd go home to make up with your pa, but you never showed up."

Everything clicked into place in Jeff's memory when he heard the name Sam Houston Gossett, and tears streamed down his cheeks.

"Bill Robinson! Thank God you've jogged my lost memory. I was hurt in a fall on my way home and haven't known who I am until this very minute."

Robinson shook his head in astonishment. "Do you mean you've been wandering around all this time since I last saw you not knowing you're Sam Gossett?"

"That's the size of it. I've been going by the name Jeff Barber."

"Let's get out of this crowd, son, and you can tell me all about it."

Sam wasted no time on details but gave Robinson a brief account of where he had been and what he had been doing. "Enough about my wanderings," he said. "Tell me about Pa and the rest of the family."

"Sammy Rose is trying to walk, and Mary's second is a boy. Your pa had another stroke and is helpless. Can't speak nor move except for one hand. The other's paralyzed, along with his legs."

"And Gretel?"

"It's a hard life for her and your brothers and sisters."

"I'll go home at once," Sam told Robinson. "It's a good thing I brought my horse and my gear and a change of clothes."

"Is there anyone who should know?"

"I need to find Sean O'Hara from Fort Worth and explain why I'm leaving. He knows me as Jeff Barber, but he knows about my memory loss. He'll understand."

"Go find him." Robinson laid a hand on Sam's shoulder and turned him in the direction he needed to go. "Be on your way, and the Lord go with you."

When Sam caught up with O'Hara, he grasped his hand in both of his and explained how he had recovered his memory. "Thanks for everything. I'm leaving right now and will get to Fort Worth ahead of you and that wagonload of goods. I'll collect the rest of my belongings and say goodbye to your family and to the Thompsons. Then I'm going home just as fast as I can get there."

"Can you find your way?"

"Yes, it's a long ride from here, but I remember the way. Had I only known when I came through Comanche that I was Sam Gossett, I could have headed west and been home long ago."

"Will we see you again?" O'Hara asked.

"I don't know. It'll take me a spell to stitch together my two identities. Now that I'm Sam again, I don't think I can be Jeff any more." Sam gave O'Hara a hug. "I'll never forget you and all you've done for me."

After a brief stop in Fort Worth, Sam rode hard toward Coleman County, pondering his future. For too long he had drifted like a leaf in the wind; now he was ready to anchor in one spot--home. Anxiety weighed heavy on him. Would Pa still be alive? Would he forgive him? Could Gretel ignore his past insolence? Could he put his life as Jeff Barber and his feelings for Sophie and Molly behind him and pick up the threads of his real identity?

Day after day he traveled, stopping just long enough to rest his horse, refill his canteen, eat a few bites of the grub Mrs. O'Hara had packed for him, and sleep a few hours in his bedroll.

Southwest from Fort Worth he rode across rolling prairie dotted with occasional live oaks and cottonwoods, then across low hills through cedar brakes and shinnery. He crossed the Brazos, then the Paluxy, allowing Chance to drink his fill at each stream. The trail became more difficult as it wound between hills into the open areas of Erath County across meadows covered with prairie grass.

The further he rode toward home the more he realized that he could not return to his life as Jeff in Fort Worth nor to Sophie and Cal at the Lazy Hawk. He would cherish the memories, but they were just that--memories. He was a Gossett born and bred, and the place he was headed was where he belonged. He was not the boy Sam Houston Gossett who had sneaked away from home to drift through life at the wind's will but a young man ready to rejoin his family and assume responsibility for them.

Mesas sat like giant tables in the distance as Sam rode among rolling hills spotted with low cedars and rocky outcrops. The days on the trail brought a variety of scenery: scrub oak, prairie grass, the occasional settler's cabin, stock tanks, goats, and cattle.

Sam marveled that Robinson had been the key that finally unlocked his memory and set him on the road home. From the storehouse of jumbled memories, he kept coming back to the moment of truth when he recognized Choctaw Bill and knew that he was Sam Houston Gossett.

As he rode into Brown County, open fields flattened among the mesas, and scatterings of mesquite brought the familiar feel of home. He crossed Blanket Creek and Salt Creek, through meadows of prairie grass and low hills spotted with cedar and live oak, and continued westerly into Coleman County past Santa Ana Mountain toward his destination. To travelers from afar the landscape appeared harsh and unforgiving. Certainly it lacked the beauty of East Texas pines and the grandeur of South Texas oaks draped with Spanish moss, but to Sam it was the most beautiful sight he had ever seen--home.

Finally he arrived at the Gossett place and closed his eyes for a moment to blot out the signs of neglect. The garden was spotted with weeds and an uneven pile of wood waited to be chopped. Charred mesquite stumps squatted in the pasture waiting to be pulled up so the land could be cultivated. A tear tickled down his cheek as he thought of what might have been had he not run away.

Gretel was hanging clothes in the yard. She saw him and came to meet him, both hands extended. "Is it really you, Sam? Welcome home."

"Gretel, I'm so sorry. I'm here to help. Just feed me and let me sleep in the barn. I'll work hard around the place."

"I prayed you'd come." Their hands touched in a clasp that brought back Sam's old longing for her.

He tore his eyes from her gaze and said, "Can I see Pa now?"

"You'll find him much changed. He can't speak but answers questions by blinking his eyes. Twice means yes, once means no."

"He may not want to see me."

"Don't worry. He forgave you long ago. He's given you up for dead and will be happy to see you alive."

Gretel waited outside while Sam slowly opened the door and went in. Pa sat in a rocker, one hand trailing useless at his side and legs motionless beneath a multicolored, hand-pieced, patchwork quilt.

"Pa, its me, Sam." He took his father's useless hand in his, and a tear coursed down the old man's cheek.

"I'm sorry, Pa. I understand now that you were trying your best to keep the family together. It was me tearing us apart, but I'm home to stay if you'll let me. Please say it's all right."

Pa blinked twice and took Sam's other hand in his good one with a grasp no longer firm. Then he dropped Sam's hand and pointed to his Bible lying on a small stool beside him. Sam placed it in his lap and watched him fumble with his one good hand through the worn pages. Pa's shaking finger found the verse he wanted in the 15th chapter of Luke and pointed.

Sam stooped down and read aloud, his voice choking with emotion: "For this my son was dead, and is alive again, he was lost and is found." He embraced Pa, and a feeling of peace flowed through him. At last he was home, no longer spiteful and resentful, no longer drifting.

In the months that followed, Sam directed all his energy into improving the neglected Gossett homestead. He pulled stumps and cultivated a field. The soil began to produce a better yield, and the small herd of stock fattened and reproduced. He kept a discreet distance from Gretel, but she was never out of his thoughts. Pa seemed to be fading away. He lost weight and let his food spill out of his mouth and down his shirt when Gretel or Polly Sue tried to feed him.

One night as Sam lay sleeping in the barn, Gretel came to wake him. "Your pa's had another fit of apoplexy, Sam. I've sent James for the doctor, but it's no use. He's unconscious and gasping for air like every breath will be the last. Polly is sitting with him, and she's scared, poor child."

Sam rose and pulled on his pants. "I'll come with you to see if there's anything I can do." Together they went to the house and walked to the alcove that served as the bedroom. As they approached the bed, Ben Gossett, husband and father, gasped several times and fell silent. Sam checked for a pulse and shook his head. Then he ran his hands across his father's eyelids and closed his eyes.

Gretel brought warm water and washed the body, then for the second time in her young life dressed a husband for burial. The family took turns sitting with Pa for the remainder of the night. The next day they buried him in the family plot next to little Bertie and the stillborn infant.

Not long after Pa's funeral Sam drew Gretel aside as she went to the hen house to collect eggs. "I'm sorry for the way I acted to you and Pa. He was right to marry you to keep the family together. I know you've had a hard row to hoe."

"He was a good man, Sam." Long pent-up tears streamed down Gretel's face.

Sam enfolded her in his arms with her head resting on his shoulder as she wept. "I know. My behavior was childish and jealous. I was smitten by you from the first moment I laid eyes on you at Ft. Croghan. Now since I've been home my feelings have deepened, and I want more than anything to take care of you. Will you consider marrying another Gossett?"

She stepped back from Sam's embrace and laid two fingers against his lips. "Shh--it's too soon."

"I know," he sighed.

Then Gretel took his hand and smiled through her tears. "Perhaps--some day."

EPILOGUE

A year after Pa's funeral Choctaw Bill rode up to the Gossett homestead and viewed with approval the tidy yard and the bedroom Sam had added onto the house. Gretel greeted him in her best Sunday dress refurbished with new ribbons and lace.

The family gathered in the front yard for the ceremony, and Gretel carried a bouquet of mixed flowers from the garden. Rose stood up with Gretel, and Matt was Sam's best man. Mary cuddled the babies, and the rest of the family joined her in a semicircle facing the wedding party. A half dozen neighbors and their children rounded out the spectators.

After their vows were spoken, Gretel served cider and kuchen all around.

"I've waited a long time," Sam whispered.

She smiled at him, blue eyes filled with promise. "I know."

* * * * *